JESSICA BECK
THE DONUT MYSTERIES, BOOK 48
# DONUT DESPAIR

D1521458

1

The First Time Ever Published!
Donut Despair
The 48th Donuts Mystery

Jessica Beck is the *New York Times* Bestselling Author of the Donut
Mysteries, the Cast Iron Cooking Mysteries, the Classic Diner Mysteries, the Ghost Cat Cozy Mysteries, and more.

WHEN JAKE TAKES A MISSING person case near the North Carolina coast, Suzanne decides to tag along for a bit of a "vacation." There's no time for her to rest once they get there, though, when they get embroiled in a small town's present as well as its past, and they must unravel the mysteries surrounding it before murder books its own stay there.

To Sandy James, Constance Meadows, and Diane Minsker.
Three former English teachers of mine, each one worthy in her own
right to claim part of the credit for what I've become, and absolutely
none of the blame,
And as always,
To P and E.

## Chapter 1

I HEARD A CREAKING sound coming from the attic above me, and I clutched the recently discovered golf club tightly in my hands as I made my way toward the stairs of the old house in the middle of a dismal night. The club wasn't much as far as weapons went, and I would have much rather had my trusty softball bat—thick and heavy and reassuring—in my grasp, but I couldn't be too choosy.

After all, I was in a strange place—a very long way from home—and there was an ominous tension in the air that I'd sensed from the moment we'd first arrived.

Was the noise upstairs simply rooted in my overactive imagination, or was there real danger lurking there for me? I thought about trying to call Jake again, but I knew that cell phone reception in the house was spotty at best, and with the wind and the rain pounding and pulsing outside, I knew that there wasn't a chance I'd be able to get through to him.

I could always grab my rain jacket and boots and take my chances outside, but I wasn't in the mood to be pushed around, forced out into the gloom of a night like tonight, not by the weather, or *whatever* might be waiting for me upstairs.

"You'd better be ready for me, because I'm coming up," I said bravely as I mounted the first step and made my way upward.

Chapter 2
Earlier That Day

"SUZANNE, I'VE GOT TO leave town for a few days, a week at the longest," my husband, Jake, told me as I was closing Donut Hearts for the day. I'd had a steady influx of customers despite the fact that the Re-NEWed rebuild was getting started next door, putting a severe cramp in my customers' parking-space access. I'd resigned myself to the fact that I'd be working in a construction zone for the next several months when Jake had dropped in and told me this latest development. "I've got an interesting case in Parsons Pond near the Outer Banks, and they need me right away. They're even putting me up in an old house near the water while I'm there. Is there any chance you'd be able to join me?"

Since Jake had started his detective consulting business after retiring as a special investigator for the North Carolina State Police, I'd been promising to tag along on one of his cases, but so far it hadn't worked out. "I'm sorry, but I can't. Sharon Blake is heading to Spain in a few days, so Emma would have to run the shop all alone." Emma—my assistant, a college student, and a very dear friend—worked at the donut shop with me four days a week, and when her mother was in town, they ran it two days together without me. That left one day for me to work the shop solo, something that Emma had *never* done. She had expressed zero interest in tackling it during several of our past conversations about the possibility of her taking the helm alone, and I couldn't really blame her. It was a lot of work soloing at Donut Hearts.

"Okay, I understand," he said, clearly a little disappointed that I wouldn't be going with him.

"I'll come with you one day. I promise," I said as I touched his cheek and smiled.

He returned it. "I'm holding you to that. Who knew that a donut shop would be such a demanding business?"

"If I had to guess, I'd say that *anyone* who's ever worked in one, run one, or even watched a show about one on television would think so," I said as my grin broadened. "When are you leaving?"

"My bag is already packed, so since I'm soloing, I'm going to head out right now."

"Be safe, and let me know when you get there," I said as I kissed him good-bye.

"Try to stay out of trouble yourself," he replied.

"I'm probably not going to get into much mischief here making donuts," I answered.

"Maybe not, but we both know that's not *all* you do."

"You don't have to worry about me. If anything happens in April Springs while you're gone, I'm staying out of it," I answered him.

"Suzanne, don't make me promises you can't keep," he replied.

"Okay, how about if I promise to at least *try* to stay out of trouble while you're away?" I offered.

"That's the best I'm going to get, so I'll take it," he said. "I'll keep you posted."

"Do that, and drive safe," I said.

"I'll do my best, but I don't have any control over what the other maniacs on the road might do."

"I'm glad you qualified that by saying '*other* maniacs,'" I replied with a laugh.

"You know what I mean."

"I do," I said, my broad grin evidence that I was just teasing.

To my surprise, not three minutes after he left, Emma came into the shop, clearly distressed about something. "What's going on, Emma?"

"It's my mother. She can't go to Spain after all."

"Why not?" I asked. Her mother was quite a world traveler, though she never went with her husband on any of her adventures. Ray Blake owned and operated our local newspaper, the *April Springs Sentinel*, and there was no way he'd ever leave his baby, his first love, in someone else's hands.

"Her best friend just came down with the flu. At least they both had traveler's insurance," she said.

"Does that mean that you'd both be free to run the shop for a few days, maybe even a week?" I asked her.

"Mom would love it, and so would I," she admitted. "Where are you off to?"

"I'll let you know in a second if I'm going anywhere," I said as I pulled out my cell phone and called my husband. Hopefully he hadn't gotten too far yet, and if he still wanted me, I was going to finally follow through with my promise to join him on one of his jobs.

"What's wrong? Miss me already?" he asked when he answered my call, and I could hear the smile in his voice.

"You know it. How far have you gotten?" I asked.

"I'm still in town," he admitted. "I figured I'd grab a bite at the Boxcar while I could. You never know what you're going to get in a strange place. Why? What's up?"

"Sharon's trip was cancelled, so if you still want me, I'm game," I said.

"I'll pack a bag for you right now," he said enthusiastically.

"Slow down there, Skippy. I'll pack my own bag, if you don't mind. Finish your lunch, and I'll meet you at home. I shouldn't be more than five minutes."

"Better yet, I'll have Trish hold my order and we can eat together," he countered.

"I thought you were in a hurry to get there," I reminded him.

"I am, but a detective has to eat, doesn't he? And so does his wife."

"I'll be there as soon as I can get away," I said.

He hesitated before hanging up. "Thanks, Suzanne. This means a lot to me."

"It will be fun," I said.

"Even with me working on a case?"

"I plan on going to the beach and soaking up some sunshine," I said. "*You're* the only one who's going to be working."

"It's going to be great having you there with me. See you soon," he answered happily.

Emma had to have been eavesdropping. "You're going on a trip to the beach? Mom's going to be so jealous."

"Are you sure she won't mind pitching in?"

"Are you kidding? It will give her a chance to add to her travel funds," Emma said. "Go have lunch with your husband. I can finish up here for you."

"But it's not even your day to work," I protested.

"Consider it a bon voyage gift," she said happily. "Now go before I change my mind."

"Yes, ma'am," I said as I handed her my apron and headed across the street to the Boxcar Grill to join my husband for a last-second meal before we left for the coast.

"Look who I found," Jake said as I joined him at his table after giving Trish my order. My mother and her husband were sitting with him, and Phillip stood and held my chair for me as I sat down.

"More accurately, we found him," Momma said. "Jake tells me that you two are taking a little vacation."

"Is *that* what he called it?" I asked as Trish brought me my sweet tea. "Have you all ordered?"

"They just did," Jake said.

"Suzanne, why is a trip to the coast *not* considered a vacation in your mind?" Momma asked. She was as sharp as ever, and I knew that she'd pick up on my question the moment I presented it.

"Well, it's a vacation for *me*," I said.

"And for you?" Momma asked Jake, turning the intensity of her stare toward my husband.

"Are you working on a case?" Phillip asked eagerly. As a retired chief of police, he was always extremely interested in what my husband was up to. For that matter, Jake was a retired police chief himself. He just had a much longer resume than my stepfather did. My husband had been a state police investigator, a much higher position in law enforcement, before he'd married me and retired to April Springs.

"As a matter of fact, I am," Jake said.

"Come on, man. Give me details," Phillip urged him.

"Phillip, leave the man alone," Momma scolded her husband. "I'm sure he doesn't want to discuss it at the table."

Jake shrugged. "I don't mind if you don't. I just don't want to bring the party down."

"Is that what we're having here, a party?" I asked him with a grin.

"Some folks might call it that," he answered. "*Whenever* you two ladies are in the room at the same time, isn't that naturally the definition of a party?"

Momma reached across the table and patted Jake's hand affectionately. "You have become quite adept at that, you know."

"What's that?" Jake asked.

Before she could answer, I jumped in. "At being charming." I patted his hand myself, and then I turned to my mother. "Leave him alone, Momma."

"What did I do?" she asked with as much mock innocence as she could muster.

"I'm investigating the circumstances around a missing developer," Jake admitted.

"I didn't know that," I said. "How long has he been missing? Do they suspect foul play? Who are the suspects? Has he—or she—been up to something to make law enforcement think that there's more to the story than meets the eye?"

Momma arched an eyebrow at me. "I thought you were going for a vacation, Suzanne. It sounds to me as though you're planning to investigate with Jake."

"No, ma'am," I said quickly. "Those were just a few idle questions."

"They didn't sound all that idle to me," she countered.

Phillip spoke up. "Dot, she's just naturally curious, that's all."

It was still an odd thing to have my stepfather defend me, especially to my mother, but our relationship had come a long way over the years since the two of them had been married.

"And you know what they say that leads to," Momma answered, unfazed by her husband's comment.

"I'm not a cat, though," I said. "I'm going to stay out of Jake's business."

"Then why are you going?" she asked me rather pointedly.

"I haven't been to the coast in forever," I said, and then I quickly added, "Besides, since when do I need a reason to spend time with my husband?"

"You don't, at least as far as I'm concerned," Momma said approvingly.

We would have probably been fine if Phillip hadn't decided to interject himself into the conversation again. "Need any help, Jake? I'm free."

"You really shouldn't invite yourself along on their trip, Phillip," Momma scolded him.

If he was upset by her comment, he surely didn't show it. "For all we know, Jake would love to have me tag along," Phillip said.

"I'm afraid that you've put him in a rather awkward position, dear," Momma told her husband.

"You're right. Sorry about that, Jake," Phillip answered, duly chastened.

"It's not that I wouldn't love having you," Jake explained, "it's just that they're stretching the budget as it is bringing me on board. I'm not even entirely sure who's covering my fee."

"If it's about the money, you wouldn't have to pay me," Phillip offered.

He was really eager to go; that was obvious.

I looked at my husband and shrugged, letting him know that it was entirely up to him. If he wanted to invite my stepfather along, and my mother as well as far as that was concerned, I wasn't going to veto the move. After all, we'd had a bit of luck working together in the past. Maybe it would be fun.

"Well, if you're really that interested, let me make a quick call," he said as he pulled out his cell phone.

"Jacob, you'll do nothing of the sort," Momma insisted. "Phillip, we have something scheduled in two days, need I remind you?"

"I forgot all about the wedding," Phillip said glumly. "Can't we get out of it?"

"We cannot," Momma insisted. "It's your goddaughter, for goodness sake! You're giving her away!"

"I hate wearing a suit," he said a bit sullenly.

"Even though you look quite handsome in it," Momma said. "There will be other trips."

"Promise?" he asked as though he were twelve years old.

"I'm sure of it," she said, and then she turned to us. "When are you leaving?"

"As soon as we eat and I can throw a few things into a bag," I said just as Trish brought a large tray with our food on it.

"Enjoy, folks," Trish said as she delivered each plate to its rightful owner.

I grabbed my cheeseburger and took a bite. No surprise: it was amazing.

When I glanced at my mother, I saw that she was watching me closely. Was I about to get another lecture on manners? I finished chewing and then swallowed before I spoke. "Are you going to eat that pickle?" I asked her as I pointed to her plate.

"I am," she answered. "If you'd like one, order it, Suzanne."

The diversion had worked, and I had somehow spared myself a scolding, so the day was looking up. After all, what could be better than going to the coast and having a nice little vacation while my husband found a missing developer?

If only it were that easy. But even at that moment, I had an inkling what was in store for us when we got to Parsons Pond.

## Chapter 3

"WHAT EXACTLY DO YOU know about this case?" I asked Jake as we headed out of town. "Surely they've told you more than just that a developer is missing." We had a seven hour drive ahead of us, so there would plenty of time for us to chat. As a matter of fact, knowing my husband, as soon as we arrived at Parsons Pond, he'd be so wrapped up in the case that there wouldn't be any time for me at all. That was fine. I could use the opportunity to explore the area, take long walks on the beach, and catch up on some of the quiet time I'd been missing lately.

"The details are sketchy, but I've been told that the developer is a bachelor in his early thirties. He comes from money, and evidently his mother owns half the downtown area of Parsons Pond."

"That somehow sounds familiar," I said, thinking about Momma and how much of April Springs she actually owned. Even I didn't know. My mother liked to keep things close to the vest, but I knew from first-hand experience that she was worth a small fortune, maybe even a large one. Some folks in town thought *I* was rich by association, but as my bank balance surely attested, that was far from the truth. Sure, after Momma was gone, I'd probably get a chunk of it—she'd hinted at as much in the past—but I'd rather be dirt poor and have her around than have all the money in the world but no mother, and I'd take that deal ten out of ten times.

"Maybe as far as that part goes, but I understand Mrs. Sandler uses her money like a club to get her two children to toe the line. Evidently it worked with Hank, the missing developer, but his sister, who goes by Sissy, oddly enough, is a different story. She's a bit of a wild card. These days, about the only thing the mother and daughter agree on is that they're both worried about Hank."

"You said that he was single, but are there any significant others in Hank Sandler's life?"

"He just broke up with someone, but there's a chance he was already seeing someone else on the side. Evidently the developer has been quite a playboy in the past," Jake admitted.

"How about business? From my experience, developers can get themselves into all kinds of deals with some shady people."

"He's supposedly clean. The only side business he's had is a restaurant he owned up until three weeks ago," Jake said.

"What happened to that? Did it shut down?"

"No, evidently he sold it to his former best friend for a song," Jake replied. "Supposedly it was doing pretty well, too."

"Why would he do that?"

"That's one of the things I need to find out," Jake said as he continued driving. We were going due east, and the sun was now overhead. At least the rest of our journey would give us the sun at our backs and not in our eyes. "Suzanne, I hope you don't regret joining me."

"Why would you ask me that?"

"I'm going to be tied up, so you're going to be left to your own devices, at least until I can figure out what happened to Hank Sandler."

"I'm a big girl, Jake. I was amusing myself long before you came along, remember?"

"I don't doubt it for one second," he said. After a few minutes of silence, he added, "I'd ask *you* to help me investigate, but I don't think it would go over very well given my conversation with the chief of police. He seems to be old school all the way, and I got the impression that he's not all that pleased to have my help. My guess is that hiring me wasn't his idea."

"If it wasn't the chief of police, who do you think was behind it?"

"If I had to guess, I'd say it was Eloise Sandler, Hank's mother," Jake said.

"That makes sense. She could have hired a private investigator and bypassed the police altogether, though." That was what I would have done if I had a lot of money and a missing loved one.

"Maybe, but if she did that, then she'd be directly involved," Jake countered. "My guess is she wants to keep as low a profile in all of this as she can. I've got a meeting with her this evening after I check in with Chief Vickers, and it's her house we'll be staying in when we get there."

"We're going to be staying with someone else?" I asked, unable to hide my disappointment. That wasn't exactly good news, at least as far as I was concerned.

"Not in her home," Jake reassured me. "One of her rentals happens to be free. I'm guessing that she lives in a much more opulent place than where we'll be staying."

"Do you think there's any chance our place will be facing the ocean?" I asked.

He shrugged. "The address is on a slip of paper in my wallet. Look it up on your phone."

I did as he suggested, but what I found didn't help matters. "Jake, you said Parsons Pond, right?"

"Yes," he answered.

"Not Parsons Beach?"

"No, I'm sure that it's Parsons Pond. Why?"

"Parsons Beach is on the water. Parsons Pond is thirty miles from the ocean," I said. "According to what I'm reading here, the only body of water besides a small pond in the town is a swamp."

"I didn't know that," Jake said apologetically. "Do you want to change your mind?"

Visions of walking on the beach disappeared in a flash, and so did some of my enthusiasm for the trip, but I'd meant what I'd said. I was coming to be near my husband. Everything else was just a detail. "No, it's fine."

"It's not too late to change your mind," Jake offered.

"We're over halfway there now. What could you do, pull over and have me hitch a ride back to April Springs?" I asked with a laugh. "This will be fine. We'll *make* it fun."

"Are you sure?"

"I'm positive," I said, trying to put a bright smile on my face for him.

"Good. I didn't relish the idea of turning around at this point," he admitted. "I'm guessing there will still be plenty for you to do once we get there."

"You bet," I said. I put my phone away. After all, I was afraid if I uncovered any more bad news, I'd be even less willing to tag along. Still, we had the drive to the coast—or at least near the coast—and the trip back, and I wasn't about to waste any of it. "Gabby's foreman on the ReNEWed rebuild next door is quite an odd bird."

"Really? Tell me about him."

"His name is Darrel Masters, and unless I miss my guess, there's more going on there than a professional relationship between them."

"Gabby is dating her contractor?" Jake asked.

"I don't know if they've gotten that far, but I saw them together this morning, and she was definitely being more friendly with him than usual."

"For Gabby, that wouldn't take much, though, would it?" Jake asked me with a slight smile.

"Gabby's okay," I said, defending my friend to my husband for some odd reason. "You just need to get to know her."

"Maybe you're right. Exactly how long does that take?" he asked.

"I'm not sure. I'll let you know when I get there," I said with a laugh. "Honestly, she's not that bad."

"High praise indeed," Jake said. "Still, Gabby hasn't had much luck in the romance department over the years, has she?"

"About as much as Trish has," I said, thinking about the Boxcar Grill's owner and operator. "Still, I found you, so there's hope for my friends."

"Suzanne, do I need to remind you that I came into your life because of a *murder*?" Jake asked.

"No, but I'm confident the universe would have found a way to bring us together even if that hadn't happened."

"Do you really believe in fate?" Jake asked me, clearly curious.

"I'm not sure on the whole, but I do know one thing: we belong together," I said. "How it happened isn't nearly as important to me as the fact that it did happen."

"I agree with that much, anyway," he said.

The hours seemed to fly by, but it was dark by the time we drove past the city limits sign of Parsons Pond. I made a promise to myself that I'd make the most of the experience. So what if there wasn't a nearby ocean? There was a decent-sized town, and I'd have plenty of time to explore it. While Jake was off looking for the missing developer, I'd have a chance to see another corner of the world that was brand new to me.

It was something that I planned to embrace.

At least I felt that way until Jake followed the directions to the house where we'd be staying.

When we first saw the rental, I wondered if it was too late to back out after all.

"It's a bit dreary, isn't it?" Jake asked me as we stepped out of the truck.

I decided not to react to the understatement. "I'm sure it will be fine," I said. "Do you have the keys?"

"They're under the cast iron cow," he said.

"Where exactly do we find that?"

"I was told that it would be on the back porch," Jake said. "Should we grab our bags or have a look around inside first?"

"I want to make sure we can get in before we bring in our things," I said.

We walked up the back steps together and onto the screened porch that looked out over a large expanse of darkness. It would be morning before we saw exactly *what* we'd be looking at, but at the moment, what I was interested in was seeing the inside.

There was a yellow light on in back—no doubt to keep the bugs from swarming at night—and it illuminated the space with an eerie golden light. The porch sported a variety of cast iron animals, from pigs to chickens, and indeed, cows, too. A metal Guernsey the size of a small cat was among the other animals. It sported faded black spots on a weathered white background, and Jake lifted it up to see if anything was under it.

At least the key was there, as promised.

Maybe the inside wouldn't be as dreadful as the outside looked.

One could only hope, anyway.

"It's not that bad," Jake said as he flipped on the kitchen light.

I begged to differ. Faded wallpaper, torn in places, adorned the walls, and the owner had used the lowest-watt bulbs available, casting everything in dark shadows. The furniture was heavy and ornately carved, dark from years of neglect, and the hardwood floors looked to be scratched and gouged beyond repair. All in all, it wasn't the homiest place I'd ever been in, not by a long shot.

"And she rents this out? To tourists?" I asked.

"I doubt they get all that many tourists this far from the coast," Jake allowed.

"I can't imagine living here very long."

"A year's lease would probably feel like a very long time," Jake agreed. "I'm sorry I got you into this, Suzanne. This was supposed to be a fun trip for both of us."

I couldn't let Jake accept the blame for something over which he had no control. "At the very least, it will give us a story to tell when we get back home. I'd take some photos to send Momma, but I'm afraid there wouldn't be enough light to do it all justice."

"I've already barked my shins twice," he agreed with a smile. "Maybe we should get some kneepads while we're in town. Speaking of which, I'm supposed to check in with Chief Vickers and then pay a visit to our hostess, but I don't have the heart to leave you out here all by yourself."

"Nonsense. I'll be fine," I said. "Let's grab our bags, and by the time you get back, I'll have us settled in." My words were braver than my spirit, but I wasn't about to let Jake see just how much this place gave me the creeps.

"Are you sure?"

"I am," I said as we walked out to the truck together to grab our bags.

Once we were back inside, he kissed me lightly. "I'll see you soon. Thanks for being such a trooper. Is there anything I can bring you from town?"

"How about some hundred-watt lightbulbs?" I asked with a smile.

"If I can find any, I'll buy them out," he agreed.

I watched from the porch as his headlights disappeared into the night, and only when I heard something big rustling through what I could only assume was tall grass did I go back inside just as rain started to pound down.

Evidently there were scarier things outside than in.

At least so far.

The rest of the house was more of the same, only worse. The bedrooms featured four-poster beds, canopies and all, that looked as though they hadn't been dusted in twenty years, and with every step I took, the floor creaked below my feet. There was something else, too, a smell of age to the place that instinctively repulsed me. I wasn't sure I'd ever be able to get used to the aroma. Then again, if things went well for Jake, maybe we wouldn't be there long enough for that to be a concern. After all, I was counting on my husband's detecting abilities more than ever. If he could find the missing developer in short order, we might even be able to drive the last thirty miles and see the Atlantic Ocean after all.

It was something worth hoping for, anyway.

## Chapter 4

"JAKE, IS THAT YOU? I can't hear you," I said into my phone an hour later.

"Suzan...., rrrrrkkkkkddddd......," the voice on the other end said. At least that was what it sounded like to me. Either he was gargling glass, or the reception at the rental was terrible. I tried quickly moving from room to room, but it seemed to get worse with every change, not better.

".....soon," he said, and then the call died altogether.

Did that mean that he'd be back soon or that he'd be leaving soon? Then again, he could have meant that a monsoon was heading our way for all I knew. I pulled back the faded sepia curtains and looked outside. It was still raining, and hard. As I was about to turn away, a flash of lightning illuminated the night sky for a moment. Was someone out there, standing in the rain and staring up at me? The instant of light had been so brief, so fleeting, that I couldn't be sure, but it had certainly *looked* like a person to me. I'd already searched the place for a flashlight, but all I'd been able to find were a few candle stubs. Then again, I hadn't gone upstairs to the attic or down the steps into the basement.

I was brave, but I wasn't that brave.

Looking around the living room, I'd found an old golf club leaning in one corner. Grabbing it, I made my way back to the window, hoping for another flash of light so I could tell what I'd really seen out in the yard.

Rain was still pounding down, and the wind was howling, but so far, there was no more lightning.

Then I thought I heard a sound coming from the attic.

Calling out to give myself a false sense of bravado, I started up the stairs. Had it been the natural creak of an old house in a storm or something more ominous? Surely no one was up there. Or were they?

*Suzanne, get ahold of yourself. You're a grown woman. You've faced down more than your share of actual killers, and now you're jumping at shadows and losing your composure over a creaking old house? You can do better than that.*

*You are better than that.*

I shouted out, "You ghosts need to keep it down up there! There are live people in the house again, and we won't put up with your shenanigans, do you hear me? You'd better be ready for me, because I'm coming up," I said bravely as I mounted the first step and headed toward the stairs to the attic.

Before I did, though, I took another look outside. I felt instantly better when I saw headlights coming toward the house.

I hoped it was Jake, but at that point I would have taken just about anybody.

As the vehicle neared, I could finally make out Jake's truck in the rain, and I felt an overwhelming sense of joy that my husband was nearly back. As he neared the house, I watched the spot where I thought I'd seen the stranger a few minutes earlier, hoping beyond reason that whoever had been there had decided to hang around.

Instead, all I saw was a weathered and stunted old tree near where I'd *thought* I'd seen the stranger earlier. Could it have just been my imagination after all? The shape and the size were both right for a person, but I could have sworn that I saw a person lurking there, not a small, gnarled old tree.

I decided at the last second to keep the incident to myself. After all, I didn't want Jake so worried about me that he wouldn't leave me alone in the house again. He had a job to do, and in a way, so did I.

My task was not to impede his investigation in any way, and I was going to see that I didn't, no matter what.

As Jake came in the back way, I could see from his wet hair and clothes that he'd been caught out in the storm unprotected. "I packed my raincoat," he said with a grin. "It's in my bag. Fat lot of good it did me. Is there any chance there are towels here, or even running water, or is that too much to ask?"

"Oh, we've got plenty of towels," I said with a smile as I put the golf club down on the table.

"Trying to get nine holes in before the storm?" he asked as he gestured to it.

"I thought I might hit a bucket of balls, but I couldn't find any," I answered, trying to downplay my earlier reason for grabbing the club. "Take your pick," I said as I led him to the hall closet outside the main floor's bathroom. Inside were what could best be described as the place old towels went to die. There were faded old pieces of cloth that looked as though they might fall apart from a single touch, but I found him a fairly new one, at least compared the others, and handed it to him. "Will that do?"

"At this point, I'll take any port in the storm," he answered with a shrug. "Is there running water?"

"Yes, and it's even warm, though hot would be a bit of a stretch," I said. "You should take a shower and get into dry clothes unless you have to go back out tonight." As I said it, I felt a small ball of fear build in my stomach. I wasn't sure I could handle him leaving me again so soon, but I wasn't about to say anything.

"About that. We've been invited to a late supper by the owner of this mausoleum," Jake said with a shrug. "I'm sorry. I tried to get us out of it, but she was insistent."

"Her son is missing," I said reasonably, though a dinner party was the last thing I wanted to attend tonight. "Of course she wants you to get started right away. How long do we have?"

Jake looked at his watch. "We've got around ten minutes before we have to leave. We might be able to make it if we hurry."

"Then go grab a shower while I start getting ready," I said. "Don't worry. We'll make it."

"You're awfully positive, given the circumstances," he answered as he followed me into what I had decided would be our bedroom for the trip.

"If you think of all of this as one big adventure, it's *amazing* what you can put up with," I answered with a smile. "Now hurry. I don't want to be late."

"Yes, ma'am," he said with a smile of relief. I'd done the right thing keeping my earlier scare from him. Even his mere presence was doing a lot to perk me up, and if we were to face this dinner, at least we'd do it together.

Our hostess's home was a true showplace, a marvel of modern engineering, and everything that our rental was not. The architect appeared to be part Frank Lloyd Wright, part I. M. Pei, and part industrial designer. Clean lines, though not always straight, swept through the open space, and whoever had built the structure hadn't been afraid of using stainless steel, beat-up old barnboard, and quarter-sawn oak in the most amazing combinations. The living/dining/entertaining area was bigger than our cottage back home, and I could see enough hints of the kitchen through oddly spaced and positioned openings to make me want to skip the party and go straight to the galley.

Eloise Sandler met us at the door, and she was nothing like I'd expected. The woman seemed to be too young and vibrant to have grown children, and she was dressed in a way that would have left my mother in disbelief, from the height of her hemline to the cutouts in her dress that made one ponder what, exactly, if anything, the woman was wearing underneath. She'd had plastic surgery work done—there was no way she could look like that at her age without it—but only her hands and her elbows gave it away. I've read that those areas, along with the neck, were the hardest things in the world to disguise from the ravages of aging, but even hers must have been lotioned and pampered beyond belief to look as good as they did.

Her voice when she introduced herself was low and sultry, as though she'd just downed a shot of whiskey and it was still burning in her throat. "You must be Suzanne. It's lovely to meet you, Ms. Bishop."

"Actually, I go by my maiden name, Hart," I said as I took her hand. It was even softer than it looked, and I was tempted to ask her what her nightly regimen was, but that was more forward than even I could pull off, though my mother might have disagreed.

"How very modern of you," she said. "I've dispensed with all of that myself. You may call me Eloise."

I felt as though I had just been given a royal boon. "You have a lovely home, Eloise," I said as I looked around in admiration.

"Do you like it? Honestly?"

"I adore it," I admitted. "I can't wait to see the kitchen."

"Then you shouldn't have to," she said, sounding pleased with herself. "Jake, if you'll introduce yourself to my other guests, I'd like to give your wife a tour of the place."

"As much as I'd love to see it, Eloise, I don't want to be a problem," I said after seeing Jake's frown suddenly appear. He'd managed to hide it almost as quickly as it had appeared, but I'd seen it, and no doubt our hostess had as well.

"It's no problem, but perhaps you're right. After we finish eating, we can take a tour then."

"I can't wait," I said.

Eloise nodded, and then she turned to her other guests, who had all been following our conversation closely while trying to pretend they weren't.

"Jake, Suzanne, I'd like you to meet my daughter, Sissy, her dinner companion, Gregory Kline, Mayor Hiram Humphries, his wife, Anna, and of course you've met the police chief, Bo Vickers, and this is his sister, Ginny."

"I still don't know why this couldn't have waited until morning, Mrs. Sandler," the police chief said a little grumpily. "Who eats after seven, anyway?"

"Civilized people do," Eloise said. "However, if you and your sister would like to leave now, feel free."

"We'll stay," Ginny said, albeit reluctantly. She was a slip of a woman, a few inches taller than me but weighing a good thirty pounds less. Her brother, the police chief, matched her lithe physique, and I had to wonder if they might be twins. The mayor and his wife resembled a bowling ball and a pin, respectively, while Eloise's daughter was an understated beauty. It must have been difficult growing up in the shadow of a woman who clearly wanted to be the bride at every wedding and the corpse at every funeral. Sissy's companion, Gregory Kline, didn't match her in any way, shape, or form, and if they were a couple in any sense of the word, I'd give up my matchmaking merit badge.

"Let's be seated then, shall we?" Eloise asked as she gestured to the long walnut dinner table, decorated, plated, and even sporting calligraphy name cards placed precisely in front of each setting. The table itself had live edges and had clearly been made from a single slab of material, with bright-white bowtie inserts holding the dark contrasting wood together. It seemed to float in the air, and as I looked for my name, I wondered if it were possible that the table was worth more than our cottage. I found my name and took my seat. I had been placed between Gregory Kline and Mayor Humphries. Across from me sat Jake, who was in turn flanked by Sissy Sandler and Anna Humphries. For some reason, Eloise seemed to be amused by the dinner party, or maybe her expression was the result of all of that plastic surgery; I couldn't say. But it was indeed an odd gathering, especially considering the circumstances.

As the first course came out, served by an impeccably uniformed couple who exhibited great skill at their jobs, Sissy asked, "Has *anyone* here heard from Hank since he's been gone?"

"Your brother's name is Henry," Eloise corrected her daughter automatically. I knew that tone, having been raised by a strong Southern woman myself.

"Nobody calls him that, Mom," she said just as routinely.

"Sissy, I've asked you a thousand times not to call me that, either," she said with a note of clear disapproval in her voice. "I am simply Eloise."

"Relax, Mom. Everyone in Parsons Pond knows how old you really are," she answered with a hint of defiance in her voice.

"Perhaps, but everyone here is not from Parsons Pond," she reminded her daughter.

"It's a fair question, Eloise," the mayor said stiffly. "Where could Hank, er, your son be? It's not like him to just disappear like this."

"I wasn't aware that the two of you were that close," she said casually, but there was nothing spontaneous about her tone.

"We've recently gotten to know each other," Mayor Humphries said diffidently. "As a matter of fact, we were supposed to meet for breakfast this morning."

"Hump, not everyone is as addicted to their day planner as you are," his wife said without a great deal of affection. "Eloise, wherever did you get that dress? It's absolutely scandalous."

"Of course it is. That's my mother's forte," Sissy said.

"Sissy," Eloise chided her, but there was no anger in it.

"It's true, Mother Dearest," she said, ignoring the plate in front of her as she turned to the chief of police. "Where is my brother, Chief Vickers? Surely you should have been able to find him by now. He's been missing since last night."

"You know Ha...Henry. Chances are he'll turn up in his own sweet time," the chief said as he glanced at his sister and touched her hand lightly. There was real affection, even compassion, in that look, and I had to wonder what exactly it had meant. "I'm perfectly capable of doing my job; I don't need any help." He then turned to Jake. "No offense intended."

"None taken," my husband answered magnanimously.

"That's not why I insisted you consult with Inspector Bishop," Eloise said. "It has nothing to do with my faith in your abilities, Chief. It's just that this might be a situation above your usual pay scale." There was an edge of steel in her voice, and the chief did his best not to show his resentment.

"Of course I'll be glad to get all of the help I can," Chief Vickers said, nodding in Jake's direction but not making eye contact with him.

"Gregory, where do *you* think my son might be?" Eloise asked her daughter's companion pointedly. "You've been remarkably quiet all evening."

"The fact is that I don't have an opinion in the matter one way or the other," he said steadily.

"But as his best friend, surely you have some idea where Henry might be."

"Eloise, you know as well as I do that we haven't been best friends since high school," he said icily. "I'm his attorney, and nothing more." He turned to Sissy. "Is that why you invited me?"

"No. Mother implied that she wouldn't appreciate me bringing you tonight," Sissy admitted.

"So of course you did exactly the opposite of what you thought she wanted. I was afraid that might be the reason," Gregory said a little wistfully. "I'm sorry it turned out to be true, Sissy." The attorney then turned to our hostess and added, "I don't have time for this nonsense. Eloise, I have a case I'm trying in the morning, and I'm going to need all of the time I can find to prepare for it. If you'll all excuse me," he said as he stood, not waiting to see if he'd be excused or not and clearly not caring one iota either way.

If Eloise minded his abrupt departure, she didn't show it. Sissy stood, and after glaring at her mother for a moment, she went off after her date for the evening. "Gregory, wait a second. Let me explain."

"I honestly don't know why I'm here, either," Ginny said. "Hank made it perfectly clear yesterday afternoon that his private business was his alone now, not mine." She turned to her brother. "I'm sorry, but I'm going, Bo."

"Hang on, Ginny," he said, but it didn't work.

As his sister headed for the door, the police chief stood. I half expected him to bow in Eloise's direction as he made his own excuse. "Sorry, but I'm her ride."

"By all means, feel free to go," she said, dismissing him.

Once the brother and sister were gone, Eloise smiled at the remnants of her party. "And then there were five."

One look at the Humphrieses, and I knew that they wouldn't leave under gunpoint, so I doubted that we'd have any more sudden departures. I had to agree with Sissy. I wasn't sure what the reason behind the dinner party had been, but whatever it was, it had surely failed.

Dinner was surprisingly ordinary and left me a bit disappointed. After everything else, I'd expected an amazing meal, but unfortunately, all of the work had gone into the presentation and very little into the taste.

The Humphrieses looked to be settling in for the evening when they were suddenly dismissed by our hostess as well. Eloise had them out the door so quickly and so smoothly that I wanted to take notes in case I found myself in a similar position in the future.

Once the staff left, it was just Jake, Eloise, and me, and I was about to say something when a yawn escaped my lips.

"Oh, dear, I've kept you up past your bedtime," Eloise said. "I honestly don't know how you manage the hours of a donut maker, Suzanne." My occupation had come up in the course of the evening's conversation, though no one had seemed dutifully impressed by my vocation and avocation.

"You get used to it in time," I said. I still hadn't gotten my promised look at that kitchen, and I was more interested now than ever.

"Forgive me, but I've kept you both here long enough. You must come again soon," she said as she took my elbow and angled me toward the door. The woman really was an expert at getting rid of her guests, and I had to wonder if she hadn't planned the earlier departures after all. She seemed a master at knowing exactly what buttons to push.

"Thanks for this evening," I said as Jake and I were ushered out into the night.

At least it had stopped raining.

"That was odd," Jake said as he drove us back to our temporary abode.

"Which part of it?" I asked as I tried to snuggle a little closer to him for warmth as well as companionship, since the evening was turning cool.

"All of it," he answered. "I'm not sure what the purpose of that was tonight, but it certainly wasn't eating."

"The food was kind of bland, wasn't it?" I asked.

"I'd rather have your leftovers than their main course any day of the week," Jake admitted.

"You say the sweetest things," I told him.

He glanced over to see if I was being sincere, and when he saw that I was, he nodded. "I meant every word of it. If that's what passes for nightlife around here, I think I'll pass on it from now on."

I nodded even as I yawned again. "Sorry. I'm still on Eastern Donutmaking Time."

"It's a good time to be on as far as I'm concerned," Jake admitted. "I'm beat, too."

"What, there isn't going to be any late-night sleuthing session with the police chief?" I asked him, dreading the chance that he would leave me again soon.

"Not tonight, at any rate. We're meeting first thing in the morning. He's picking me up at the rental, so you can have the pickup truck at your disposal tomorrow. There is no way that I'm going to leave you stranded out here without your own transportation."

"That's thoughtful of you, but will you be able to manage?"

"Don't worry about me," Jake said as he pulled into our long drive. "I don't know about you, but I'm ready for some sleep."

"I was ready an hour ago," I admitted. "I wonder if there's anything in the pantry we could nibble on before bed?" I'd given it a cursory look earlier, but now I was interested in it in earnest.

"I don't know, but I'll raid it with you."

It was not to be, though.

The moment Jake turned on the light in the kitchen, I knew that sleep wasn't going to be happening anytime soon after all for either one of us.

Chapter 5

"WHAT HAPPENED HERE?" I asked as I looked at the muddy footprints—mostly obscured by the sheer amount of caked mud in the treads—that crossed the kitchen, went through the living room, up the stairs into the attic, and then finally out the back door again.

"I certainly didn't do that earlier when I came in," Jake said as he flipped on the back-porch light again. "I never even went upstairs."

I peeked outside with him and saw that the footsteps originated and ended there. "How did we miss those on our way in?"

"In our defense, it *was* dark," he said as he pulled out his cell phone.

"Who are you calling?" I asked.

"Apparently no one. I can't get a signal on my phone. Hang on. I'll be right back."

I hadn't meant for my voice to sound so shrill. "*You're leaving me here all alone?*"

"It's okay, Suzanne. Whoever was here is long gone by now."

"Before you do anything else, let's make sure of that first, okay?" I was shaken by the disturbance more than I could express. So why was my husband taking it so casually? "Why are you being so calm?"

I wasn't exactly sure why I'd bothered asking the question. Jake had been *born* for emergencies. He seemed to thrive when chaos reigned around him, something that must have made him invaluable as a cop but that could be irritating as a spouse. After all, when I freaked out, I didn't like to do it alone.

"There's no reason to get upset about it now," he said. "Let's figure out what happened, and *then* we can decide the appropriate way to react."

"You can take that approach if you want," I chided him, "but if it's all the same to you, I'll get upset now and worry about explanations later."

My husband put his phone back into his pocket and then took my hand. "You're right. Let's make sure no one's still here."

"Thank you," I said, feeling a little guilty about raising my voice earlier. Still, if ever there was a time to feel justified doing it, it was now.

We walked from room to room, even where the footprints hadn't been. I was relieved as Jake and I peered under every bed, behind every curtain, and into the depths of every closet. When he headed for the stairs to the attic, I hesitated, though.

"What's wrong?" he asked me, clearly puzzled by my failure to move.

"The truth is that I've been avoiding the basement and the attic since we first got here," I told him.

"Suzanne, you've convinced me that we need to do a thorough search," he explained. "If you'd like to stay here, I can do it by myself, but I'm following those muddy footprints upstairs."

"No, I'll go with you," I said, though I stopped to pick up the golf club I'd found earlier along the way.

"Do you have some kind of affinity for that thing? You were holding it when I came in to tell you about the dinner party earlier."

"I thought I saw something just before you got here," I confessed.

That stopped him in his tracks. "What?"

"Right before you came back, there was a flash of lightning in the distance, and I happened to be looking out the window. I could have sworn I saw someone standing outside."

"And you didn't tell me?" he asked as he unbuckled his gun holster and pulled out his service revolver, which he always carried with him when he was on a case.

"I wasn't completely sure that it wasn't my imagination," I admitted. I knew that he was armed, so seeing his weapon wasn't a surprise at all, but I still felt better with the golf club in my hands.

After all, guns could jam, but blunt objects couldn't.

"It shouldn't matter. If you see something, and I mean anything, you need to tell me." It was more of an order than I was used to hearing from him, but he had every right to make the demand given the circumstances.

"I'm sorry," I said.

That softened him immediately. Jake put his weapon back in its holster and rubbed my shoulders. "I just don't know what I'd do if anything happened to you."

"Then let's make sure that it doesn't," I said. I felt better telling him about what I'd seen, or at least what I thought I'd seen. "Come on. Let's finish our search."

"Are you going to carry that club around with you?" he asked me with a smile, no doubt trying to lighten the somber mood we now shared.

"Hey, you have your weapon, and I have mine," I explained.

"Good enough. I understand," he said.

We walked up the steps to the attic in single file, and even though I wasn't sure what we'd find, I still hadn't expected what we saw when we opened the door.

It was a room that Emily Hargraves could have designed herself, though there wasn't a single moose anywhere in sight.

You couldn't say that about cows, though.

A large space that took up at least half of the upstairs attic had, at one point, clearly been a teenager's bedroom and living space, and that kid had been crazy about cows, Holsteins to be specific. The walls, the floor, and even the sloped ceiling—though now faded—had been painted white and covered with random black spots, and I mean all of it. A student desk and chair had both been given the same treatment, as had the dresser and the headboard of the single bed. A layer of dust covered everything, and it appeared that no one had used that particular space for years, except for the muddy footprints that seemed to head for the bed and then suddenly turn back toward the door.

"Wow. Somebody was really cow crazy," Jake said as he took the scene in.

"To say the least," I said. "Emily Hargraves would love this."

"No doubt. Let's keep searching the attic," Jake answered, getting back to business.

I agreed. I wanted this hunt over and done with so we could figure out what to do next. The other portion of the attic space had been used for storage and was currently stacked up with trunks, boxes, abandoned furniture, and anything else that could be used for storage. If someone *was* hiding up there, he or she was a master contortionist. I wrote the space off as unvisited, since the footprints hadn't gone anywhere near that part of the attic. Once the new day dawned, I'd have to come back up and take pictures with my phone. No one would believe it, and I *had* to send Emily some photos.

"Now on to the basement," Jake said.

"Lead on," I told him.

At least there weren't any footprints leading down the steps, but that didn't make the space any less creepy. What was it about basements and cellars that seemed to set my teeth on edge? As we walked around the cobwebbed, dark, and damp space, I knew the answer without even voicing the question out loud. There wasn't a door to the outside down there, but there was a bulkhead that led out, though it was clear it hadn't been opened in years.

It turned out to be another dead end.

"Satisfied?" Jake asked me once we were back in the kitchen. I noted that we had both avoided the footprints, and not just to keep from spreading the mess around.

"Not even close," I answered. "We still don't know who made those."

"I'm talking about the fact that we're alone here," he said.

"That I can agree with," I answered.

"Okay, then I'm going to go outside and make a phone call. I can't get a signal anywhere in this house."

"Who are you going to call?"

"Chief Vickers," he said. "He needs to see this."

"Jake, I'm not sure I can stay here tonight after this," I told him.

"Did you see any motels on the way in? Because I surely didn't," Jake said.

"There's got to be *someplace* else we can stay," I said.

"Let's not worry about that just yet," Jake answered in a calming voice. "Right now, we need to deal with one thing at a time."

"That's fine, but I'm going on the record right now that I'd rather sleep in the truck than stay here a single night," I told him.

"Understood," Jake said as he started to step outside before hesitating. "Are you going to be okay while I make this call?"

"I'll be fine," I said, though I wasn't at all sure it was true.

I was no shrinking violet who jumped at every shadow, but this was a very real violation of what was supposed to be our personal space. Who would do such a thing, and why? As Jake went outside to make his call, I decided to check our things to make sure everything was still there.

As I moved toward our bags, I got the oddest sense that someone was watching me.

I didn't see how it could be true, but I was glad that I had my club with me anyway.

If any ghosts or bad guys came at me, they'd have to fight off my swinging golf club, and I was going to aim for the bleachers.

"The chief is on his way," Jake said behind me, and I nearly jumped out of my skin.

"You startled me," I said as I tried to get my breath back.

"Are you telling me that you weren't expecting me?" he asked as he put his arms around me.

"Hey, I'm jumpy. I admit it," I said as I held onto him for another second.

"It's going to be fine, Suzanne," Jake said.

"You keep saying that. I just hope it's true."

The chief hadn't impressed me at dinner, but his prompt appearance at the rental house put him in a more favorable light in my mind. It didn't hurt that he glanced at the muddy footprints but didn't stop to study them as he approached me first. "Are you okay, Mrs. Hart?"

"I'm fine," I said, already getting tired of saying it. "And please, call me Suzanne."

"Good," he answered, and only then did he kneel down to get a closer look. "Jake, you said it was like this when you got back from dinner, right?"

"I certainly wouldn't have left the house like this, and if I had, we wouldn't have called you," I said. I might not be the best cleaner in the world, but I wouldn't have been able to ignore that mess whether I was late for dinner or not.

"I didn't mean to imply...I'm sure you wouldn't," he stammered.

Was he really that uncomfortable around me, or was it women in general? That might have explained him bringing his sister to the party earlier and not a wife or a date. Then again, I could just be assuming things that weren't true. For all I knew, Chief Vickers might have a handful of women waiting breathlessly by their phones for him to call. That thought made me smile, something that the chief missed but my husband caught. Jake shot an eyebrow skyward in question, but I just shook my head in response. It wasn't important, and I certainly wasn't going to mention my flight of fancy in front of the chief of police.

We heard more cars approach outside, and in no time, there were three officers busily going through the house as though it were a major crime scene. One was videoing the footsteps, one was taking samples of the dried muddy prints on swabs, while the third did an exhaustive search of the house, no matter how many times we'd protested that we'd already done just that ourselves. The back door opened yet again, and I said without thinking, "Must we really have someone else here invading our space?"

It wasn't a police officer though.

It was our gracious hostess, Eloise.

"I didn't mean to intrude, but I came as soon as I heard," Eloise Sandler said. She'd changed into slacks and a sweater, both black, and she *still* managed to look more elegant than I did in my finest moment. "Did they break in?" she asked Chief Vickers.

"That doesn't appear to be the case," he said deferentially. Almost by way of an apology, he turned to us and explained, "I thought Ms. Sandler would want to know what happened, so I called her."

"It was wise of you to contact me, Chief," she said, looking at Vickers fondly for a moment.

"If no one broke in, then they must have had a key," Jake said.

"I would say that's a fair assumption," Eloise agreed.

"This being a rental, there are probably a ton of them floating around. There are at least two keys to this place, and maybe more," I said. "We were instructed to get the one in the cast iron cow."

"There are two more hidden on the porch," Eloise acknowledged. "Let's go look and see if any of those are still there."

Jake, Chief Vickers, and I followed her back out to the porch while the rest of his team continued to work.

Eloise walked directly over to a cowbell and pulled it from the wall. Behind it, I could see another, smaller nail, where a spare key could have been easily hidden.

There wasn't one there, though.

"It's gone," she explained, and then she moved to a tin painting of, to no one's surprise, a cow standing placidly in a field staring at the artist. There was still a key there.

"May I ask what the fascination with cows is with this place?" I pondered aloud.

"I bought this house from the Bridger family," our hostess explained. "They lived in town for over thirty years, but then they suddenly couldn't live here anymore, so I bought the place to use as a rental. Their daughter, Shannon, was fascinated with cows."

"I have a friend, Emily Hargraves, who is absolutely nuts about them too, though she is mainly interested in her stuffed animals, Cow and Spots."

"Is she interested in cows only?" Eloise asked.

"No, she has a pet moose, too," I said, and then quickly added, "A stuffed animal, I should say."

"Well, it's clear that whoever was here knew about at least one of the spare keys," Chief Vickers said, trying to bring the conversation back around to a pertinent point.

"I'm at a loss about who it might have been," Eloise said.

I looked at her steadily for a moment, and then, without thinking, I asked, "Really? The more I think about it, the more I believe that there's a good chance it was your son."

"Henry?" she asked, clearly surprised by my statement. "What would he be doing here? He has a perfectly good home three miles away, and for that matter, if he needed anything, he knew that he could come see me."

"What if there's a *reason* he's gone, though?" I asked.

"Suzanne, this might not be the best time to discuss our theories," Jake corrected me gently.

He was right, and what was more, I should have known it without being reminded of it. "Please forgive me, Eloise. Sometimes my imagination gets the better of me. I probably read too many cozy mysteries for my own good."

"It's fine, dear," she said, though it was clear that I'd put something unwelcome in her mind. I felt awful about it, but there was nothing I could do at that point to ease her mind.

I stifled a yawn, and the chief spotted it right away. "I'm sorry, but my team's going to need to be here a little while longer."

"They can have all of the time they'd like," I said. I turned to our hostess. "Eloise, as gracious as you were to offer this place to us, I'm not sure I'll be able to stay here after someone broke in. Jake and I are going to have to find somewhere else to stay."

I was afraid I might offend her, but I'd meant what I'd told my husband. I wouldn't stay somewhere even at gunpoint if I didn't feel secure, and I didn't feel safe there at all. I could live with the outdated furnishings, the faded paint, even the creepy noises that pervaded the house, but having unwelcome and uninvited visitors was where I drew the line.

"I completely understand," she said quickly. "You must stay with me. I insist."

I didn't like the idea of us tripping over each other in that house either, no matter how cool it might be. "That's generous of you to offer, but..."

"I won't accept no for an answer," she said quickly. "I have guest quarters on the grounds that will suit you perfectly." Eloise had the grace to blush a bit as she added, "When I offered this place to you, it was before I got to know you. I never should have put you here in the first place. You and your husband have traveled a great distance and gone to more than a little trouble to help find my son, and I've rewarded you with lodging you *here*. Please let me make it up to you."

I was about to speak when Jake replied instead. "That's kind of you to offer..." he said, and I knew his next word was going to be a "but," so I jumped in and interrupted him.

"We'd be delighted," I said.

Jake looked surprised, our hostess looked pleased, and the chief looked bored with the whole conversation.

"Then let's leave this to the experts, shall we, Suzanne?" she asked. "Let me help you with your bags."

I wasn't about to let that happen. "I can get them," I said.

"Suzanne, do you mind if I hang around here a bit? I can get a ride back with the chief." He looked at me for my approval, knowing how adamant I'd been earlier about not being left alone. Still, he was there to do a job, not to babysit me, so I needed to let him out of my sight long enough for him to actually get a chance to do it.

"Stay as long as you need to," I said, and after I gave him a quick kiss, I grabbed my bag and turned to Eloise. "I'm ready if you are."

"Then off into the stormy night we go," she said with a warm smile as she put her arm in mine.

Chapter 6

"THIS THING COULD CLIMB a tree if it had to, couldn't it?" I asked as I stepped up into the passenger seat of the massive SUV the diminutive woman was driving. I'd seen the brand on the road before, but I'd never been in one. My idea of luxury transportation was riding around in my Jeep after getting it washed. This piece of high-tech engineering was worlds beyond what I was used to.

"I suppose so, though I've never tried it. Shall we test the theory right now?" she asked me with a wicked little grin. There were times I could swear Eloise forgot that her son was missing, and then others when I could see the fear and tension fight to break through. Was all of this lighthearted bravado just an act, or did she perhaps know more about her son's whereabouts than she was willing to let on?

"Why don't we keep it on the pavement unless we run across a tree in the road," I suggested.

"That's probably a sound idea," my hostess said. As we drove, she added, "I hope this doesn't offend you, but I think you're off base with your theory, Suzanne."

It took me a second to figure out what she was talking about. "You're talking about Hank."

"Henry," she gently corrected me. "He wasn't in that house tonight."

"What makes you so sure of that?" I asked her as she deftly wheeled the tank-like vehicle down the road toward her home.

"He wouldn't go there, of all places," I said.

"Why not? It seems to be as good a place as any to me if he didn't know Jake and I would be staying there tonight."

"That's where you're wrong. I told you earlier about Shannon Bridger, the teen who was obsessed with cows? She lived in that house long ago, but what I didn't tell you was that my son dated her all through high school. For years, he and Shannon were quite the item, and many folks thought they'd go away to college together and end up getting married someday. That was not to be, though."

"Why didn't it happen?" I asked Eloise as I studied her in the low light from the dashboard.

"He and Shannon evidently weren't as good for each other as people around here seemed to think," she said.

"How did *you* feel about her? Was there bad blood between the two of you?" I asked the question without thinking, not meaning to be cruel to my hostess but honestly curious about her reasoning.

I braced myself for a scolding when Eloise surprised me by laughing. After it subsided, she explained. "The truth of the matter is that Shannon was probably too good for my son, not the other way around, if that's what you're thinking."

"I don't believe I've ever heard a mother say that the person her child was dating was too good for them," I admitted.

"That's because you didn't know her. Shannon was special. Every boy in that school had a crush on her, including Gregory and Bo, but she only had eyes for my Henry. Shannon was *always* one step ahead of the curve, at the top of every class she ever took. She was destined for great things, but then the day after they all graduated from high school together, she vanished, and no one ever heard from her again. Henry was devastated, and frankly, I'm not sure he's ever gotten over her." It was a stark confession, and it told me more about the woman I was with in a few choice words than I had learned since we'd first met. "I thought that giving him the Bridger project to rehab and sell would be good for him, a way to finally get closure, but it might have finally been what drove him over the edge."

"What does Sissy think about all of this?" I asked her.

Instead of answering my question, she asked me one of her own. "What do you think of my daughter, Suzanne?"

"She certainly seems confident," I said carefully, not wanting to make another misstep.

Eloise laughed. "That's probably the perfect word for her. Sissy might not know where she's going, but she certainly travels there with great self-assurance. Her internal compass might be off, but her drive certainly isn't."

"She and Gregory Kline aren't really dating, are they?"

"No, though I wouldn't mind the match. Sissy is more attracted to the bad boys of Parsons Pond, at least what passes for bad around here. I had hopes that Gregory's friendship with Henry would become a motivation for him to date my daughter, but alas, they don't see it that way. Perhaps Sissy is right. Gregory surprised me when he bought the pub from Henry for such a low amount recently. If you ask me, he took advantage of their former friendship at a time when my son was vulnerable. I have no idea what Henry was thinking. If he'd come to me, I could have found a handful of other suitable buyers and made him quite a bit of money on the deal, but his days of consulting me on business matters apparently are over."

"That sounds to me like there's more than the pub sale that's bothering you," I said, and then sat in silence to give her time to decide if she was going to expand on that comment or not. I'd learned over the years that most people would talk to fill a void in the conversation if you just gave them enough time to start to feel uneasy about the lull. Keeping my mouth shut had been a difficult lesson for me to learn, but I had finally mastered it.

Well, mostly anyway.

Sure enough, after what felt like forever but was most likely not much more than a minute of silence, she spoke again. "Henry is not only trying to break away from me financially but emotionally as well. I thought he was going to settle down, eventually take over my business, marry someone like Ginny Vickers, and ultimately give me a few grandchildren. Alas, none of that is going to happen based on his recent behavior. This vanishing act he's pulling is just the latest in a long line of actions that have left me more than a bit perplexed."

"How serious was he with Ginny?" I asked. "Was the breakup really just yesterday?"

"Why do you ask that?" she queried as we neared her property.

"Ginny's reaction at dinner was obvious, wasn't it? The wound is clearly still fresh. I had hoped to talk to her privately about the rift, but she didn't stay long enough to allow that to happen. Maybe there's still a chance they'll work things out," I said, trying to give the woman at least a bit of encouragement. So far, she'd had a pretty bad couple of days, so if I could lighten her load just a little with some hope, whether false or not, it might help her get to sleep tonight.

"No, I'm afraid the damage he did cannot be undone," she said. "From what I've heard secondhand, he called her a mindless cow with no spirit. She was devastated, and the police chief was angry enough to confront my son on the town square two days ago. The two of them, along with Gregory and Shannon, were all thick as thieves in high school, but after Henry went away to college and Shannon disappeared from all of our lives, things were never the same between Bo and the others."

"When you say confront, what exactly do you mean?" I asked, marveling at how well the police chief and my host had gotten along that evening, both at the dinner party and at the house.

"He wouldn't dare lay a hand on my son, if that's what you're asking, but everyone knows what a temper Bo had in school. I thought his time in the military had broken him of the trait, but evidently he gave Henry quite a tongue-lashing. Perhaps it would have escalated into something else, but I came along at that point and defused the situation."

"How did you manage to do that?" I asked her.

"I simply reminded each of them of how much they had to lose by continuing their very public behavior, and both men ultimately saw reason."

I had a feeling there had been more to it than that, but I wasn't about to press her on it any further. Eloise Sandler was clearly a woman who liked to use her position, her power, and her money to get her way, and anyone in her debt would, sooner or later, feel the weight of the burden when she started making requests that were clearly much more like demands.

"Well, we're here," she said as she put the car in park and shut off the engine.

"I see your house through the trees, but where is the guesthouse?" I asked her.

She stepped outside in a rare lull in the rain, and I followed her. There was a path there that I'd missed upon our arrival, mostly because it had been bathed in darkness, but as we approached it, a string of lights on either side of us lit up as we moved forward. We were fifteen feet from a looming structure when the path lights led to an even brighter set of outdoor lights. As they lit, I could suddenly see where Jake and I would be staying while we remained in Parsons Pond.

The guest cottage had clearly been designed by the same architect who had created the main house, though there were enough different elements to give it its own distinct feel. The A-frame construction, sporting slanting exterior walls that met in a peak at the towering roofline, was enveloped in warm spotlights that lit up the exterior. I hoped those lights could be turned off manually once we were inside, because otherwise, I wouldn't get a second's rest inside. As Eloise opened the front door, the lights inside came on automatically. "Don't worry. There's a manual override switch to make all of the lights operable. I just didn't want to fiddle with light switches when I came out here myself."

"Do you use this space often? I hate the thought that we are evicting you," I said as I looked around at the dark cherry wood. Not just the beams were made from the lustrous wood but the furniture itself. The walls between each section of the A-frame's massive beams had been painted white, in stark contrast to the darker wood. At first, I thought the filler spaces were just made up of painted drywall, but upon closer examination I could see that they were planked pine boards, whitewashed to make the beams more dramatic.

It worked.

"It is a refuge for me usually, but now it's just for you and your husband," she explained as I continued to look around.

We were standing in a comfy living/dining/kitchen space, and a staircase in back led to an expansive loft that covered half the main floor. The rest of the steeply pitched walls towered above us, forming a massive cathedral ceiling, and a chandelier hung down to illuminate the conversation area. Instead of sleek steel, the light fixture had been created out of what appeared to be a massive tree root that had lights interwoven through the varnished tendrils.

"That must have been one massive cherry tree," I said in awe.

"How astute of you," she explained. "It was my favorite tree on the property when I was a child, and when lightning hit it and nearly destroyed it, I decided to build this space with whatever wood could be salvaged from what was left. It was an explosive strike, and we found bark and debris fifty feet from the base of the tree. For a split second, it appeared that the entire property was on fire in a white-hot heat that consumed everything it touched. My ears rang from the explosion! At least the children were away at school," she added. "I was here alone."

"So you had this built to preserve the memory of the tree you loved," I said, stroking a sanded and varnished beam with a light touch. It was almost as though you could feel the spirit of the wood itself.

Eloise nodded. "I had an inkling that you would understand. Suzanne, you and I are kindred spirits. I can feel it."

"I'm honored by the comparison, but I'm just a simple donut maker," I said.

"We both know that you are much more than that," she said softly, and after a moment, she seemed to awaken from a trance. "Let me give you the grand tour. I'm afraid it won't take long. The place is modest in size and scope."

"I think it's absolutely perfect," I told her, and I meant every word of it. The lines were simple, almost austere, and even most of the fixtures sported clean lines. I wouldn't have traded it for the main house even if I'd been given the chance. Jake was going to love it too, and I couldn't wait for him to see it, whenever that might be.

After the tour, Eloise said, "Sleep well. If you need transportation while you're here, I'm sure we can find something for you to drive."

"Thanks for the offer, but Jake's letting me drive his truck. He's going to ride with Chief Vickers."

She looked surprised. "Are you comfortable with that arrangement?"

"His truck isn't really all that much different from my Jeep," I told her, "and I'm most at home behind the wheel of that."

"Then I'll leave you to it," she said. I walked her to the door, and she paused before going back outside. "Suzanne, I do hope your husband is able to smoke my son out of hiding. I don't think he's met with foul play, at least not yet, but I have a bad feeling about this, and it's growing with each passing minute."

"Jake is good at what he does," I said, trying my best to assure her. Why wouldn't it? It had the added benefit of being true.

"As are you, no doubt," she said, and then she was gone.

I got myself settled in upstairs in the place's only bedroom, but I had no idea how amazing the view was until I turned off the interior lights and saw Eloise's mansion in the distance.

It was all certainly an upgrade from the broken old house we'd been offered earlier, but I couldn't help wondering if Hank had made those footprints or someone else had.

Either way, why had the intruder come? What had he been looking for? Had he found it, or would he be back to search again? And where was the missing son if that hadn't been him? Was he gone of his own free will, or was there something darker that explained his absence? My mind was a whirl of thoughts as I closed my eyes.

Maybe Jake would have at least some answers when he got to the guesthouse.

I had promised myself that I'd try to stay awake until he did, but that turned out to be impossible.

I didn't stir again until I felt his familiar weight settle down beside me on the bed and he kissed my cheek lightly.

I hadn't slept all that soundly until then, but knowing that he was there with me, safe as could be, took away the last worry I had, at least for the night.

As far as I was concerned, all was right in the world.

Tomorrow was indeed another day, but for the moment, I had everything I needed.

I woke up before my husband, which was no real surprise. Not only had I gotten to bed earlier than he had, but I was also on an odd schedule that, most days, had me getting out of bed before anyone in their right mind would ever do so willingly. I silently got out of bed, and Jake didn't even stir beside me.

Getting dressed quickly, I headed down the steps and made my way into the small but extremely serviceable kitchen. After I figured out how to make the coffee, I walked around in the living room area and marveled at how nice it must be to afford a place like this as a getaway. Small LED lights lined each of the beams, and once I found the switch, I turned them on to give me enough light to see by but hopefully not enough to wake my husband up. I held my coffee mug close as I curled up on the couch and just enjoyed my surroundings. It was indeed quite a step up from the place we'd been all set to spend the night in before.

Whoever had broken in and tracked that rental house up with muddy footprints had done us a favor.

I wondered if Jake had had any luck figuring out who it had been or if they'd even managed to track down the missing developer. No, he would have woken me if that had happened. I was sure of it.

I heard noises upstairs, so I got Jake a cup of coffee too and climbed up to join him.

He was already in the shower, so I made the bed and was waiting for him when he came out of the bathroom, dressed and ready to face the day.

"Coffee?" I offered.

"Thanks," he said as he took it from me and downed a big gulp.

"There's not much in the way of groceries in the pantry, but I could probably throw something together for breakfast if you'd like me to," I said.

"I appreciate the offer, but the chief will be here any second. I can't believe I slept in."

I glanced at my watch and saw that it was just a few minutes past seven. For most people, that would be way too early, but for my husband, I knew that it was true. "Will you at least get something out?"

"We're eating at some diner in the heart of town," Jake said. "It's close to the police station, and Bo says it's not bad."

"So, it sounds as though the two of you have made friends," I said as I sipped a bit of my own coffee.

"Why do you say that?"

"Last night it was Chief Vickers, and today it's Bo. You do the math," I added with a grin.

"It's just easier calling him by his first name," Jake explained as a car horn sounded in the drive.

I looked out and saw the chief was as good as his word. "Your ride's here." I'd thought about calling the police chief his date, but I decided Jake didn't have to hear *every* funny thing I ever thought. Keeping a few things to myself would probably be the best for both of us.

I followed him downstairs, and he was almost out the door when I suddenly remembered that I'd be driving his truck. "Keys!"

He paused and then chucked his truck keys to me. "Sorry. I forgot," he said with a grin.

"No worries. Happy hunting," I told him.

"You bet," he answered, and then he was gone.

I had a few choices. I could lounge around the A-frame and take it easy, but that wasn't my style. I could take a shower and get dressed myself and then head up to the main house to see what my hostess was up to for the day, but I'd already imposed in her life enough as it was for the time being.

That left the third and best option. I'd still get showered and changed, but then I'd head into town in Jake's truck and see the sights. I'd also have to find breakfast along the way. I found myself hoping that Parsons Pond had more than one eating establishment, because I wasn't all that keen to sit at a table alone next to the chief and my husband.

Surely there would be someplace else I could go.

It was funny how that ended up working out, because I never dreamed where I'd be before the hour was up.

Driving into town, I made my way down Main Street, going slowly to take in the shops. Much to my surprise and delight, I stumbled across a shop that made me instantly homesick.

It was named Donut Land, and the moment I spotted it, I knew where I'd be having breakfast that morning and probably every morning we were in town.

Chapter 7

WHEN I WALKED INTO the shop, though, I saw that there were no donuts in the display case. The owner must have been in back, because he came out at the sound of the bell over the door that announced my presence. He was a trim older man with a head of gray hair and a concerned expression on his face. "Sorry, we're having some trouble today," he said forlornly.

"I can see that. Is there anything I can do?"

He looked surprised by my offer. "Unless you know something about a Warner 750 deep fryer, I don't think so."

"This must be your lucky day, then, because I happen to be an expert on them," I said. At first I thought it was a crazy coincidence that we used the same brand and style fryer in our respective donut shops, but then again, it wasn't all that unusual. After all, there hadn't been that many choices available thirty years ago.

"Don't mess with me, young lady. I've had a bad day proceeded by a bad week and a bad month, too. I'm just about ready to trade this place for a car and then drive it off the nearest cliff."

"Don't do anything that rash just yet," I said. "I'm Suzanne Hart, owner and proprietor of April Springs, North Carolina's very own Donut Hearts."

"I'm Harley Haskins. Is there really such a place?" he asked me.

"I can show you pictures," I said as I brought out my phone. I'd taken plenty of shots during my last remodel, and I was rightfully proud of my little shop.

"I'll take your word for it. Follow me," he said as he led me into his kitchen.

His place was set up quite a bit differently than my shop was, but all of the integral components were there, including, much to my envy, a dishwasher.

"What's it doing?" I asked as I studied the fryer.

"It's what it's not doing that's the problem," he said. "I've checked the switch, the breaker, and everything else I can think of, but it just won't come on."

"How long have you had this place?" I asked him as I ducked behind the machine.

"About a month," he said. "I thought running a donut shop in my retirement sounded like fun. Boy, was I ever wrong."

"Give it time," I said as I opened a panel someone had covered with a safety flyer. I flipped the internal breaker and heard an exclamation above me.

"It just came on! What did you do?"

"There's a breaker under here within the unit itself. Get down where you can see, and I'll show you so you can do it next time."

I lifted the paper and showed him the switch. "I never even saw that before," he said, the amazement clear in his voice.

"How could you have? Why don't we get this out of our way?" I suggested as I pulled the safety warning off the machine.

"I'm all for it," he said. "There's still a problem, though. I haven't made any donuts yet, and I don't have time to make any now. The day's a total waste."

"Let me guess. You make yeast donuts and not cake ones, right?"

"Yes, I thought it would be too complicated to learn both methods at the beginning. I chickened out and stuck with yeast donuts for now."

"Well, if you're up for it, I'd be happy to give you a crash course in cake donuts right now. What do you say? Do you have an apron I can borrow?"

"I can't pay you anything," he said reluctantly.

I wasn't about to desert him in his time of need. "You're in luck, because the first lesson is free. Where's the nearest grocery store, unless you happen to have eggs, sugar, and milk on hand? I'm assuming you have flour, but how about baking powder?"

"I just bought a dozen eggs yesterday for my breakfast, and I have plenty of sugar and milk for the coffee. There's probably some baking powder left over from the last owner."

"Then we're nearly there. Point me to the flour, yeast, and salt, and we can get started."

Half an hour later, just as the oil came up to temperature in the massive fryer, we were ready to drop in the first of our freshly made donuts. Once the first batch of cake donuts was out, he tasted one the moment it was glazed. "Wow, these are really amazing."

"Thank you, kind sir. You saw how I did it. They aren't that hard. I make all kinds of donuts with that basic batter. Pumpkin is my favorite, but chocolate is really good, too."

"It sounds like a lot of work to make so many options," he said.

"Far from it. After you make a big batch of the basic batter, you just separate it into smaller bowls, and then you can make just about any kind of cake donut you can imagine."

He was dropping more donuts into the hot oil when the front door chimed. "Would you mind taking that tray out for me and see what they want?"

I laughed as I grabbed the fresh donuts I'd just made. It might not have been much of a vacation in most people's minds, but for me, it had been exactly what I'd needed to feel at home in Parsons Pond.

When I saw my husband on the other side of the counter, the look of shock on his face was worth every bit of work I'd done that morning.

"Suzanne, what are you doing here?"

I put the tray in the display case as though I'd done it a thousand times at this shop and then turned and grinned at Jake. "I thought I'd see the sights while we were here."

"So naturally you came to the only donut shop in town first thing," he said.

"Why are you even surprised? Care for a donut?" I asked him. "How about you, Chief?"

"Thanks, but no thanks. I've had his donuts before," Vickers said.

I grabbed him one and plated it. "Those were his *old* donuts. Try one of these. He made them just this morning." I was stretching the truth a bit, since what Harley had mostly done was watch, but I wasn't about to let the police chief disparage the work of a fellow donut maker.

He took a small bite, and then a larger one. "Hey, that's pretty good."

"Told you," I said. "How about you, Jake?"

"Thanks, but I just had breakfast. Is Haskins around, or did he leave you here alone to run the place by yourself?"

"Hang on. I'll get him."

I didn't have to, though. Harley came out with another tray of freshly glazed cake donuts. "I've already eaten two, Suzanne! I just can't stop myself. They are amazing." He looked up at Jake and Chief Vickers. "Hey, Bo," he said with no emotion, and then he turned an inquiring eye to my husband.

That was the perfect time for me to step up and make the introductions. "Harley, this is my husband, Jake Bishop. Jake, this is donut maker extraordinaire Harley Haskins."

"And former police chief for Parsons Pond," Vickers chimed in.

"You didn't tell me you were a retired police officer," I scolded Harley.

"The key word there in that sentence is *retired*," he told me and then turned to the man who had to have been his replacement. "What can I do for you, Bo?"

"We were wondering about the last time you saw Hank Sandler," the current chief said formally.

"I told you everything yesterday, and I don't have anything else to add," Harley said a bit curtly.

"Do us all a favor and tell me again for my partner's sake," Vickers said.

It seemed to me that Harley was about to decline when he finally thought better of it. "Fine. I don't see what it could hurt. Hank cut me off in traffic two days ago. He nearly took out my front bumper, and it took everything I had not to hit him with my car. He was in some all-fired hurry to get somewhere, and he nearly killed me doing it."

"What happened then?" Vickers asked him.

"He got out, saw that I'd missed hitting him, and then jumped back into his car and took off before I could say a word."

"What did you do then?" Jake asked him, using his full-on cop voice.

"I thought about following him, but then I remembered that I was a donut maker and not a cop anymore, so I went home and took a nap. End of story."

"Do you have any idea where he was going in such a hurry?" Jake asked.

"None. I didn't ask, and he didn't tell me."

"What time did this occur?" Jake followed up. "And where exactly was the incident?"

"It was right out front there, and it happened at twelve minutes past twelve. I'd just closed the shop for the day, and I was on my way home. Running a donut shop is hard work."

"I close at eleven," I chimed in.

"Ms. Hart, no one cares about your store hours," Chief Vickers said, clearly frustrated by the former chief's lack of cooperation.

"Speak for yourself," Harley said as he turned to me. "Don't you lose customers that way?"

"How many folks come in between eleven and twelve now? Have you ever actually counted them?"

"No, but I doubt it's more than two or three," he admitted.

"There you go. Your time is worth more than that, Harley. When do you open?"

"Five a.m. rain or shine," he answered.

"Push it to six, and you'll be happier that you own a donut shop," I told him.

Chief Vickers had clearly heard all that he was willing to take. "And that's the last time you saw him?"

"It is," Harley said, barely glancing at the chief as he said it. "Now, if you'll excuse me, I've got six more dozen donuts to fry. I've got to tell you both that I don't appreciate you coming into my business and questioning me like I'm some kind of common criminal."

"You know the drill, Chief. These questions have to be asked, no matter how uncomfortable it might be." Chief Vickers turned to my husband and said, "Let's go," but clearly Jake wasn't ready to leave just yet.

"Having fun?" he asked me.

"I'm having a blast," I told him with a grin.

He laughed as the chief coughed for his attention. "See you around town."

"Not if I see you first," I said with a smile.

"Sorry about that," I told Harley as soon as my husband and Chief Vickers were gone. "Jake was just doing his job."

"Suzanne, you don't have to apologize for your husband to me," Harley said. "We can't control what our spouses do or how they act."

"Jake just wants to find Hank," I said. "Do you have any idea where he might be? Is there a chance something bad has happened to him?"

"There's a pretty good chance, if you ask me," Harley said, surprising me. He hadn't hinted that he had an opinion one way or the other with Jake or Chief Vickers, but it hadn't taken much to get him to admit as much to me.

"Why is that?"

"Hank Sandler has made quite a few enemies over the last few weeks," Harley said.

"Including you?" I asked him gently.

"I'm not his biggest fan, if that's what you're asking. I don't believe the rumors, but that doesn't mean I have to like them."

"What rumors are those?"

Harley started to tell me, but then at the last second, he must have reconsidered. "It doesn't matter. One way or the other he'll turn up soon. Now about those cake donut varieties you make. The pumpkin donuts intrigue me. Do you use pumpkin pie spice in them, or do you add real pumpkin to the batter too?"

"Both," I said. "That's one donut question I answered. Now it's your turn to answer a Hank Sandler question."

He looked at me and frowned. "Is that how this is going to be?"

"Come on," I said, cajoling him lightly. "You were the police chief here, and it's clear you have your suspicions. I'm just asking you to share some of them with me."

"I thought you were a donut maker by trade," he asked me, skirting my proposition.

"I am, but I've been known to dig into a crime or two on the side from time to time," I admitted. It was kind of nice not being back in April Springs. There, pretty much everyone knew of my penchant to get involved in murder investigations, but in a way I had a clean slate in Parsons Pond.

"Fine," he said, "but I'm not answering any questions I don't want to. As much as I appreciate your help, I won't be dragged back into that world. My heart attack nearly killed me, and it was from the stress of the job and thinking about crime around the clock. I can't afford to risk my health again."

"I'm sorry. I didn't know. Listen, forget I asked you anything. You don't have to give me a thing in return. I offered you my services and expertise without any strings, and that's what you're going to get. I can write a few recipes down for you if you'd like."

"That would be amazing," he said with a grateful smile. "Let me just fry up the last of the donuts, and then I'll take over the front. Do you mind hanging around and working the register for me while I'm in back?"

"Are you sure you trust me out here all alone?" I asked him with a grin.

"If there's one thing I picked up as a cop, it was knowing who to trust and who not to."

"And which kind am I?" I asked him happily.

"I think you already must know that. Thanks."

"You're most welcome," I said.

Half an hour later, Harley was finished in back. He didn't have to worry about doing the dishes with that fancy dishwasher of his, so he was free to take over. While he'd been frying up the rest of the treats we'd made, I'd had a steady stream of customers. A few had grumbled about the lack of yeast donuts, but most had been delighted with the change of pace the cake donuts offered. I could see Harley's business picking up quite a bit once he switched to making both types of donuts and not just focusing on one.

Once we were alone, he said, "Listen, I'm sorry I was rude to you earlier."

"When was that?" I asked. "I hadn't noticed."

"Suzanne, you gave up your time and talent for me, but when you asked me for help, I refused. That is not the man I am. I'm ready to talk if you've got the time."

"I don't want to stress you out," I said.

"You won't. Hank has been up to a few things lately that have gotten the entire town wondering about him. He sold his pub to Gregory Kline for a song, and folks have been wondering if Greg had something on Hank that made him give it up so cheaply. They used to be thick as thieves, but after high school, that all changed. There's been a tension between them since, and I've wondered if there might be something going on there a lot darker than a pub sale."

"How about Hank's love life?" I asked.

Harley's face blanched at the mention of it, and I regretted having to ask the question. "He dumped Ginny Vickers recently, something Bo has taken pretty hard. I can't say that I blame him. The man broke his little sister's heart. Gregory was upset with him about that, too. Ginny's a nice girl, and Hank just threw her away like she was yesterday's newspaper."

"Was there someone else in Hank's life to make him dump Ginny?" I asked him.

Harley's lips pursed for a moment before he said, "That was the rumor I was referring to earlier. I don't believe it for one second, but some folks believe Hank was messing around with a married woman."

"Anyone in particular?"

He didn't answer, and I didn't press, so I decided to change the subject. "What about Mayor Humphries?"

"You get around, don't you?" Harley asked me. "How do you know the mayor?"

"I met him at dinner last night," I admitted.

"That would be at Eloise Sandler's dinner party," he acknowledged.

"You know about that?"

Harley laughed, though there was no joy in it. "You're kidding, right? The entire town knows about it," he said. "That makes you and your husband the talk of Parsons Pond."

"It wasn't all that much of anything special," I said, trying to downplay it.

"The fact that you were invited in the first place automatically makes you one of the elite around here," he said.

"That's kind of crazy."

"Maybe so, but it's the way things are. Is there anything else you want to know? I'll answer anything I can as best I can. I owe you at least that much."

I put a hand on Harley's arm just as the door opened. "You don't owe me a thing. It's been my pleasure being here all morning with you."

"That's not something you want to see," the young and vivacious woman who walked in said. "Who might you be, and why are you touching my husband's arm?"

Oh, boy. It appeared that, without even meaning to, I'd done it again.

Chapter 8

I AUTOMATICALLY PULLED my hand away. "I'm so sorry. I was just telling Harley how much I enjoyed working with him this morning," I said. I extended the same hand to Harley's wife and smiled my brightest as I added, "I'm Suzanne Hart. Your husband had a donut-making emergency, and I just happened to be passing by."

She took my hand as briefly as possible and then withdrew it just as quickly. "Oh, you're the detective's wife."

"I like to think that I'm a great deal more than that, but yes, I answer to that as well," I said.

"Delia, Suzanne has been a great help to me. Not only did she troubleshoot my fryer, but she made a batch of cake donuts that are so good they will break your heart. Try one."

As he held one of our treats out to her, she frowned. "You know I don't like those things." Wow, was she a pretty pretty princess. She must have been twenty-five years younger than her husband, and from the look of her, I'd guess that she was about as high maintenance as a woman could be. Her refusal was an insult to both of us, but Harley seemed to take it in stride. I had a feeling that he'd grown used to swallowing his own feelings for some time. "What's the latest on Hank? Has he turned up yet?"

"I wouldn't know. I'm not the police chief anymore," he reminded her.

"Maybe not, but we both know that Chief Vickers couldn't find his own car keys without your help. That's why he hired some stranger from out of town." She turned to me and added, "No offense."

"Why should I be offended by that? I'm from out of town, too," I said, having to fight harder that time to force a smile.

"Bo Vickers is a good cop," Harley said.

"We'll have to agree to disagree on that," Delia said. "Call him and see if there's any news."

"Delia, he was just here forty-five minutes ago, and there wasn't any news then," Harley explained.

"He was *here*? *Why*?" She was clearly upset by the implication.

"He wanted to question me about what happened when Hank cut me off in traffic a few days ago," he explained.

"And that was *all* that he wanted to discuss?" she asked him severely.

"That was it."

Delia seemed to take that in, and then she turned back toward the door.

"Where are you going?" he asked her.

"What choice do I have? If you won't find out for me, then I'll just have to do it myself," she replied. "I won't let these rumors continue and stand idly by while my name is being dragged through the mud."

"Nobody's doing that," he said, but it was half-hearted at best, and what was worst, he had said it to her retreating back.

Once she was gone, Harley was a changed man. The bright and energetic donut maker seemed to lose his spirit entirely with his wife's departure. Almost in a haunted voice, he told me, "Some folks think Delia was seeing Hank, but I know it's not true." Nearly as an afterthought, he added in a soft voice, "At least I hope it's not."

I couldn't stand seeing him like that. Trying my best to smile, I said, "I'm sure it will all work out. Now if you'll excuse me, I smell distinctly of donuts. I'm going to go grab a quick shower back at the place we're staying."

"I understand," he said. "Suzanne, why don't you let me split the money I took in today with you? It's only fair that you're rewarded for your hard work."

"I wouldn't dream of it," I said as I took off the apron and handed it to him. "I had a good time." I took one of the order pad sheets and jotted down my cell phone number. "If you need anything else, you can reach me at this number."

"I'll try not to bother you again on your vacation," Harley said with a slight smile. I was happy to see him get at least some of his pep back.

"I'm not talking about right now, though you can call me while I'm here if you'd like. If you need advice, recipes, or just to talk to another donut maker, give me a call." I extended my hand. "It was nice meeting you, Chief."

He smiled. "Thanks, but it's just Harley these days, and that's the way I like it."

"Then Just Harley it is," I answered.

As I headed back to Jake's truck so I could go back to the guest cottage and grab a quick shower, I marveled about how much our selection of spouses could make or break our lives. My time with Max, my first husband, had been painful most of the time, and I'd felt my spirit sag more than I'd liked. While everything with Jake wasn't perfect, it was close enough for me, and I relished every moment of our time together.

I just hoped things worked out for Harley and his donut shop in the end, but I wasn't going to put any money on it. Owning and running a donut shop was hard enough when you knew what you were doing.

If you were struggling to find your way, it made things a thousand times harder, and if you didn't have someone else's support, it could all be overwhelming.

I was on my way back to Eloise's guesthouse when I remembered the cow room in the attic I wanted to photograph for Emily. Pulling Jake's truck down the driveway, I was glad I knew where the supplemental keys were, or at least one of them. I probably should have gotten permission from Eloise or even the police before I went in, but I knew they had wrapped up their investigation of the break-in the night before, or they wouldn't have been out interviewing the donut maker. That left my hostess. Surely she wouldn't mind if I took a few quick photos. I'd tell her about what I'd done afterward, but I felt silly calling her just to get her approval first.

The police chief had evidently replaced the key behind the tin painting of a cow on the porch after he'd unlocked the door. I was glad to see it there, since I suspected that the cowbell key as well as the cast iron cow key were both still gone unless Eloise had replaced them.

I unlocked the back door, and while I was still thinking about it, I returned the key to its rightful place. After all, there was no further need for me to have one. I planned on taking a few photos and then getting out of there. While I was still on the porch, I took a couple of close-ups of the cows featured there, but I'd wait and show Emily all of them at once. I looked off into the distance and saw the house was perched on the edge of a swamp, and I was glad yet again that we'd relocated, no matter how troubling the motivation to move had been.

The inside of the house was just as gloomy at eleven in the morning as it had been the night before when we'd discovered the muddy footprints.

At least they were gone now, I was relieved to see. Evidently after the police had finished their investigation, someone had taken the trouble to mop the floors. I doubted Eloise had done it herself. She seemed more like a delegating type of woman rather than a "grab a bucket and mop" kind.

I glanced into the rooms on my way up the attic stairs, noting that daylight had done nothing to help the ambience of the space.

As I made my way up the stairs, I thought I heard something coming from the room above me.

What was it with this creepy old house and noises it made at all times of day and night?

I couldn't wait to get my photos and then get out of there once and for all.

When I opened the attic door, I could swear that I felt the whisper of death on the back of my neck, even though I knew that it was most likely just a drafty old house coupled with an overactive imagination.

I still wished that I'd had the foresight to grab that old golf club on the way up the stairs, and I held my breath as I opened the door, not sure what exactly I might find there.

"Hello? Is anyone here?"

No one answered, but that didn't mean anything. I looked around the attic room and saw that it wasn't in the same shape it had been when I'd left it the night before. Had the police and Jake made the mess while they'd been investigating after I'd gone home with Eloise, or was this more recent? The bed, along with its headboard, was pulled away from the wall, and what appeared to be a false panel behind it was now open.

I glanced in the space, but it appeared to be empty.

At least now, anyway.

I was about to take another step into the room when I heard something behind me. It was a slight creak, and it might have been the house naturally settling, but it didn't feel that way to me. I had a couple of options. I could brazenly explore the rest of the space and confront whoever might be up there with me, or I could leave as quickly as I could and let Jake and Chief Vickers handle it.

Actually, there was a third option.

I pulled out my cell phone, ready to call my husband, when I remembered that there was absolutely no cell phone service in the house. I was now back to two options, neither one of them particularly desirable. Still, leaving and calling for reinforcements was the best of a bad set of choices. I hated it when I was watching a movie and the heroine did something I considered monumentally foolhardy by pressing her luck when there was no real reason for it. I might have acted rashly a time or two in the past myself, but this was not the time for a risk I didn't need to take.

As quietly as I could, I got out of there and nearly ran down the steps, trying to get out of the house before whoever was up there tried to stop me, grabbing the old familiar golf club as I fled.

I didn't stop once I was out onto the back porch, either. I kept running toward Jake's truck, trying again and again to get a signal on my phone.

Just before I made it to the truck cab, I finally got a single bar.

I didn't want to risk losing it by getting into the truck and driving away. Besides, if someone came out the back, I'd be able to see them coming, jump in the truck, and get away.

If they weren't armed with a gun, anyway.

"Jake, where are you? I need you."

"I'm at our guest cabin. Where are you? What's going on?"

"I was just up in the cow room in the attic, and I could swear someone was up there, too," I said.

"Get away from there now, Suzanne," he said urgently.

"I might lose the signal, and I want to see who's up there."

"Now!" he commanded.

I was starting to do as I was told when I heard the front door of the house slam.

"They just left!" I yelled, abandoning my plan for a safe exit and racing toward the front of the rental house. I hadn't seen a car anywhere when I'd driven up, so most likely, whoever was there was on foot. Either that or they'd parked far enough away not to be spotted. That alone told me that they were up to no good.

"I'm going after them," I shouted into my phone, but when I glanced back at it, I saw that it was dead.

The signal had dropped again, and I was, for all intents and purposes, alone.

I ran around to the front of the house, nearly out of breath from the sudden exertion, wielding my golf club as though it was Thor's hammer or Babe Ruth's bat. I was more than prepared to defend myself from any attack or onslaught.

But whoever had been upstairs was already gone.

Jake drove up in a Prius faster than I thought those hybrids could go. He spotted me, slammed on the brakes, and jumped out, barely waiting to come to a complete stop.

"Fancy wheels. Where'd you get it?"

"Eloise loaned it to me," he said. "Why didn't you leave like I asked you to?"

"I *had* to see who it was," I told him, bracing myself for a fight. I was all for self-preservation, but I wasn't going to take myself away from potential harm every single time things got a little dicey, either. There was a fine line, and I was doing my best to toe it.

Jake must have seen the set to my jaw, because he dropped his question immediately. "Did you see who it was?"

"No, they were too quick for me."

"Should I go after them?" he asked.

"You can, but whoever it was is probably long gone by now."

"What were you doing in the house in the first place?" he asked me once he got his own heart rate under control.

"I wanted to take a few photos of Shannon's old room for Emily," I reminded him.

"Did you get them?" he asked me.

"No, I was interrupted before I had the chance."

"Then let's go take care of that now. I want to have a look around myself."

It wasn't going to happen, though, at least not right away.

We were on the front porch, ready to go inside, when three cars came up the driveway in single file. It almost looked like a parade, and I might have laughed if I hadn't recently come so close to confronting a trespasser, and possibly someone who was much worse, just a few minutes earlier.

## Chapter 9

ALL THREE DRIVERS STOPPED their cars and approached us.

"What's going on?" Jake asked them. "Did you all come together?"

"I don't know why they're here, but Mom told me you were heading over here in a rush, and I wanted to see if it might have been my brother breaking into the house again," Sissy said. "Did you see Hank?"

"No, but *someone* was here," I told them. "Whoever it was got away before I could see who it was."

"What were *you* doing here, Suzanne?" Chief Vickers asked me.

"I was getting some photos of Shannon's old room for a friend of mine," I said as though it was the most natural thing in the world for me to be doing. "How about you?"

"I was due to pick Jake up, and Eloise told me where he'd gone just after Sissy left," the chief said.

"That just leaves you, Gregory," Jake said as he stared at the attorney.

"I was supposed to meet Sissy at Eloise's house when I saw her jump into her car and drive away. Naturally, I followed her, thinking there might have been some development about Hank." He looked at Sissy and asked, "Did you forget about agreeing to meet with me today?"

"When I heard that someone was over here again, I decided to see who it was for myself." She added almost as an afterthought, "Besides, you were just going to chew me out again about dinner last night, so I figured I wasn't really missing all that much."

"As a matter of fact, it was about something else entirely," he said. "We have business to discuss."

"I don't see how that's even possible," Sissy said as she looked at him oddly.

"I'd really rather do this in private if it's all the same to you," the attorney said softly.

"It's not, though," she said. "I want you to say it in front of them. I might need witnesses later," Sissy added with a wry smile.

"Fine. Have it your way. I've got some papers for you to sign, and then I'll be on my way."

"Papers? What papers?" she asked, clearly curious about what the attorney was up to.

"Everyone in town was quick to assume that when I bought the pub from Hank at a substantial discount, I did it for my own gain, but the truth is that was what he insisted that it look like."

"Do you mean there was more to it than that?" Sissy asked softly. The rest of us didn't matter. This conversation was strictly between the two of them now.

"I was buying it for you, Sissy," Gregory said.

She was taken aback by the news. "What? That's ridiculous."

"That's what I told your brother, but he insisted we do it this way, and he wouldn't listen to reason from me. I told him that it would be better if he just sold it to you directly or even made a gift of it, but he insisted, for reasons of his own, that we handle it this way."

"That doesn't make any sense," Sissy protested as she studied the papers after taking them from Gregory. "I couldn't come up with that much money, anyway. There's no way I could afford even the reduced rate he charged you."

"You don't owe a cent on it," the attorney explained. "Upon Henry's instructions, I waited until the sale of one of his other assets came through to tell you what he'd done. He wanted you to have it free and clear, Sissy."

"Something has happened to my brother, hasn't it?" she asked him woodenly.

"We don't know that," I said as I stepped forward to comfort her.

"We do. That's what this is about," Sissy said, nearly breaking into tears. There was no persuading her that she was wrong, maybe because I wasn't entirely sure that she was myself. "He knew he was going to die," Sissy said, "and he wanted to take care of me one last time."

"That just doesn't make sense," Chief Vickers said. "How could he know that he was going to die?"

That was when a thought occurred to me, something I most definitely should have kept to myself, but I blurted it out without thinking it through. "If he was going to kill himself, then he'd know," I said, and I instantly regretted it the moment the words left my lips.

"Hank would *never* do that," Gregory said adamantly.

"I'm not so sure. He's been so lost lately," Sissy answered softly. "I thought he might finally be putting Shannon leaving him behind him, but being here just brought it all back again. We talked about her the night before he vanished."

I hadn't heard that before. "What exactly did you talk about?" I asked.

Sissy took a deep breath and then explained, "He said that he'd never be able to understand in a million years how she could just walk away from him like that. I reminded him that she'd left all of us, not just him. Shannon and I had been like sisters, and she never said a word to me about leaving, either." Sissy stopped and looked at Gregory and Bo. "Did she say anything to either one of you?"

Bo instantly shook his head, but Gregory hesitated a moment before following suit, something I caught. "Did she tell you something, Gregory?"

"No, it wasn't anything like that," he said. "The night we graduated, though, I ran into her on her way home from the party Eloise threw for all of us. She was alone, and she was extremely unhappy about something on a night when we all felt as though we had the world by the tail."

"Did she say what was wrong?" Jake asked.

"No, she wouldn't tell me. I figured she and Hank had had a fight about something, but when I asked Hank about it later, he denied it, and I believed him."

"Then what could it have been?" Bo asked. "I remember that night. We were all so happy to be graduating and going out on our own. I don't remember Shannon being upset."

"Well, I certainly didn't imagine it," Gregory snapped.

"Easy. I didn't mean anything by it," Chief Vickers said. "Anyway, that was a long time ago. It's all water under the bridge, and it doesn't explain what's going on with Hank now."

"Did anyone ever look for her after she left town?" I asked suddenly. "I mean really look?"

"I heard her folks got a postcard or two from her after she left," Bo said with a frown. "She was heading off to Europe to see the world. At least I think that's what they said. Just before the Bridgers left town for good, I talked to them. They couldn't bear the thought of having their daughter turn on them and just leave like that, but Shannon had a mind of her own, and once she made it up, the whole world couldn't change it, and they knew it. They told me that she'd threatened to run and keep running the second she could."

"That was true enough," Sissy said, and Gregory nodded in agreement.

"I wonder if Hank didn't go off looking for her?" I asked.

"Why would he do that after all these years?" Sissy asked. "And even if he did, why didn't he tell Mom or me what he was doing?"

"I couldn't say," I said, "but it's in the realm of possibility. It might explain why he wanted you to have the pub and why he sold off some of his other assets. Maybe he wanted some ready cash to fund his search."

"I wouldn't even know where to start looking for her myself, and I'm a cop," Chief Vickers said.

"I have a few ideas, but they wouldn't be cheap," Jake answered. "How much did he liquidate?" he asked the attorney.

"I'm not at liberty to disclose that," Gregory answered automatically.

"Come on, Gregory. This is serious. At least give us a hint," Sissy insisted.

After a bit of hesitation, the attorney said, "All I will say is that it would be enough to live on comfortably overseas for a few months and still allow him to finance the search."

"I still don't believe it," Sissy said. "Hank wouldn't leave without telling me or our mother. Something's happened to him."

"There's another possibility," Jake said curtly.

I got the implication almost as soon as he voiced the alternative, and I decided to voice it. "Hank could have gotten the money together and was ready to leave before someone stopped him," I said. "It sounds as though it might be enough cash to tempt someone into trying to take it from him."

"Which leads us back to square one," Gregory said. "He's still missing, and we have no idea what could have happened to him."

"Maybe not, but I have a feeling that if we don't find him soon, we're going to lose our last chance," Sissy said sadly.

"Then we'll all just keep looking until we find him," I said, and no one at that moment disputed the fact that I'd just pledged to help in the search myself.

"On that note, we'll go start looking again. Are you coming, Jake?" the police chief asked my husband.

Jake glanced at me, and I nodded. I was fine now, so there was no reason for him not to continue doing the job he'd been brought to Parsons Pond to do in the first place. "Follow me back to the Sandler residence so I can drop this car off first," Jake said.

"I'll be right behind you," he said. "I want to have a word with Ms. Sandler first anyway."

"You're not going to tell her what we've been discussing, are you, Bo?" Sissy asked, clearly trying to protect her mother's peace of mind.

"Not a chance," he said. "I just want her to know that we're doing everything in our power to find your brother."

"Of course you'd want to reassure her of that," Gregory said. "She's your biggest campaign contributor, isn't she?"

"For land's sake, Greg, Hank's my friend too, just like the two of us used to be a long time ago." The disappointment in Chief Vickers's voice was clear.

The attorney stopped and put his palms up toward the chief. "You're right. I'm sorry. That was a cheap shot."

"It's okay," Chief Vickers said offering a slight nod, accepting the apology. "We're all under some stress right now."

"Just find him, Bo," Sissy said.

It clearly touched him that she'd used his first name and not his title. "We're on it," he said with confidence.

"Sissy, we need to go over some issues about the transfer," Gregory told her. "Do you have twenty minutes right now? We could do it at my office or your home, whichever you prefer."

"Let's keep things all business," Sissy said. "I'll follow you to your office."

"I'll meet you there then," the attorney said, clearly a bit disappointed with her reaction. When he saw that she wasn't following him, he asked, "You *are* coming, right?"

"Give me a second with Suzanne," she said. "I'll be right there."

"Okay. I'll be waiting," he replied.

Once everyone else was gone, Sissy said, "I heard you were a big help to Harley this morning. Thanks for doing that."

"How could you possibly have heard about that?" I asked, surprised that she'd found out so quickly. "Strike that," I added with a smile. "I live in a small town too, even if it's not this one. How do you know Harley?"

"I went to school with his wife," she answered with a shrug.

"I see," I said as noncommittally as I could manage.

She read me correctly though. "It's okay. She's a lot to take in."

"Could I ask you what most folks would consider a pretty delicate question?"

"Fire away," she said.

"Harley told me there were rumors that Hank and Delia were an item," I said.

Sissy frowned. "I can't honestly say. I've heard the whispers too, but if I had to bet one way or the other, I'd say that it probably isn't true. It's possible, though. That's a terrible thing to say about my own brother, but Delia has a way with men that dumbfounds me. How she got Harley still makes me wonder."

"And why she wanted him in the first place is even stranger," I added.

I was surprised to see Sissy's face immediately darken. "What do you mean by that? Harley's a great guy, and a good person to boot. She's lucky to have him."

"I couldn't agree with you more," I said quickly, trying to defuse the situation. "What I should have said is how on earth did they end up together? I would think that Harley could do better, quite frankly. She seemed cold to him when she was in the shop earlier, and you could tell that it must have disturbed Harley deeply."

"She wanted him precisely because he *didn't* want her, at least at first," Sissy explained. "Delia probably thought she was getting an older man for his stability, and when Harley quit his job and bought that shop, she wasn't at all pleased. That was when the rumors started. He certainly deserves better than he got."

Was it possible that Sissy was in love with the older man as well? It wasn't that unlikely, given her rapid defense of him and how she looked when she talked about him. "I think you might just be right," I said.

"Anyway, that wasn't why I wanted to hang around and talk to you. Are you still planning to go in?" she asked as she gestured to the house behind us.

"I just wanted to get a few quick photos of Shannon's room," I admitted. "I have a friend back home who absolutely adores cows, too. She'd love to see what Shannon did to the attic."

"I wouldn't mind seeing it again myself," Sissy said. "Care for some company?"

"What about Gregory?" I asked.

Sissy smiled at me. "He can wait."

"Then I'd love it," I said.

"Let's go," she replied, and we made our way into the house together.

Maybe I wouldn't even need to grab that golf club again, since I had company this time.

Maybe.

"Wow," Sissy said as she walked into the space. "I can't believe it's still like this. I helped her paint those spots," she said as she pointed to the floor. "We were worried that her mom might be upset, but Mrs. Bridger thought they were really cool."

"Were they close?" I asked Sissy.

"You bet. Hank wasn't the only one with a broken heart when Shannon took off without a word. It just about killed her mother."

"What about her dad?"

"He started drinking, and then he got really quiet all of a sudden. I heard that not long after they moved away, he killed himself. It was all so sad."

"I can't even imagine," I said.

Sissy seemed to think about it for a minute before she spoke again. "I'd forgotten all about that hiding place of hers," she said as she walked over to the bed.

"What did Shannon keep there?" I asked her.

"Her mother didn't like her having sweets, so she'd always have some kind of candy stashed away," Sissy answered, clearly living in her own past for a moment.

"Did she keep anything else there?" I asked.

"It wasn't a very big space. Sometimes she stashed other stuff in there too, though. What did you have in mind, Suzanne?"

"I've been wondering if she kept a diary," I said. "I know I did at that age."

"I did myself," Sissy said with a soft smile. "The cover of mine had a cheap dime-store lock on it and a pair of sealed lips. It said 'My Secrets' on it, but I never had much that was juicy to write."

"Mine had a bunch of ice cream cones on it," I told her.

"Care to guess what was on Shannon's?"

"I don't have to. If it wasn't cow related, then I don't want to know."

Sissy laughed. "You got it in one. It was white with black spots. She *did* keep it there. I remember now. I wonder what ever happened to it. She probably took it with her when she left town."

"Do you think there's a chance it was still here yesterday?" I asked.

Sissy looked surprised by my question. "I can't imagine. Do you think that was why someone broke in here last night?"

"I've been wracking my brain, trying to come up with some reason, and the footsteps did lead up here. Isn't it possible?"

"Maybe, but of what possible interest could what a teenager wrote all those years ago be to someone today?"

"That I don't know," I said as I took out my cell phone. "Do you mind if I take a few shots while we're here?"

"Not a bit," she answered.

I got more photos than I would ever show Emily, and after I was finished, I said, "I don't want to keep you any longer."

"You're not. Gregory will be just fine. It won't kill him to wait all afternoon for me."

"You two have an odd relationship, don't you?" I asked.

"Odder than you could possibly know. I had a massive crush on him when I was a kid, but I was always just Hank's little sister as far as he was concerned," Sissy answered. I wasn't sure if I'd offended her or not. She was just so easy to talk to that it wasn't that hard to overstep my bounds with her. "I'd better go."

"I'm sorry if I said something I shouldn't have," I apologized quickly. "I didn't mean to offend you."

"Suzanne, it would take a great deal more than that to offend me," she said with a smile. "Come on, let's leave the past to itself and focus on the here and now."

"That sounds good to me," I said.

I followed her out of the drive after we locked the place up. Sissy took a right into town while I went left back to her mother's guesthouse. Sissy was an interesting person, and if we lived closer, I had a hunch that we could be friends.

As I drove to the A-frame to get a shower and change, I wondered about everything we'd all discussed at the house. There seemed to be myriad possibilities of what might have happened to Hank, but the truth was none of us knew anything about what had really befallen the man. I decided to stick to my plans and grab a shower, then go into town to get lunch. It was about that time, at least for me, and my belly's clock was not something I'd ever been able to refuse.

## Chapter 10

I WAS SURPRISED TO find Eloise waiting for me at the A-frame when I pulled Jake's truck into the parking space.

"Did you need me for something?" I asked her as I got out. "Forgive me. I smell like donuts from earlier."

"How many did you eat?" she asked me quizzically.

"I only had part of the first one to test it. I just assumed you heard that I worked at the donut shop this morning," I admitted.

"Why on earth would I know that?"

This was getting out of hand. "Sissy knew all about it, so for some reason I assumed that you did, too. It doesn't matter."

Eloise looked at me carefully. "Now you've got me curious. How did Harley know how to find you, let alone believe that you'd be willing to help him in his folly?"

"What's the matter? Don't you like donuts, Eloise?" I asked, feeling the slightest bit miffed by her reaction.

"Me? I adore them," she admitted. "I just didn't know you were here to work."

She had a point. "I wasn't planning on it, but I visited the shop this morning and saw that Harley could use some help, so I decided to pitch in."

"How very sweet of you. I should explain myself. The reason I call his shop his folly was because he never should have retired as our police chief."

"He told me that he had a heart attack," I said. Why was I having to explain *that* to her? Surely she knew about it, being local and all.

"True, but it was a very mild one," Eloise countered. "When it happened, he decided that he'd had enough, so he married that girl and then bought the shop without consulting anyone, including her. If the shop doesn't kill him, I believe that she surely will."

"Your family is really fond of Harley, aren't they?" I asked her.

Eloise studied me for a few seconds before she answered. "You know about that, don't you?"

"Know what?" I asked as innocently as I could manage.

"My daughter has had a crush on that man for years, along with one other local fellow," Eloise said.

"You're talking about Gregory Kline," I said.

That really caught her off guard. "I've known about both of them for years, but I didn't realize that anyone else did. You must be quite observant for a donut maker."

I wasn't sure if that was meant to be a compliment or not, but I decided that I was going to take it as one. "All I can say is that I listen," I admitted.

"You do a great deal more than that. You watch too, don't you?"

"There's nothing wrong with paying attention," I amended. "Sissy confessed her crush on Gregory to me a little bit ago, but the truth is that I'm not even certain that Sissy knows she has a crush on the former police chief."

"No, perhaps she doesn't at that," Eloise admitted.

"Is she the only Sandler woman who feels that way?" I asked.

I couldn't believe it, but Eloise actually blushed a bit. "Now you're just talking nonsense," she said after taking a moment to collect herself. "He's a friend of the family. That's all."

"Sorry. I don't know what I was thinking," I quickly said. "Anyway, I came back to grab a quick shower, change clothes, and head into town for some lunch."

"I can recommend the pub, even though my son doesn't own it anymore. If Gregory has kept things the same, it should be delightful. I wonder what his long-term plans for the place are."

"You haven't spoken to Sissy, have you?" I asked her.

"Not since this morning," she admitted. "Why? Has something changed since then?"

"Quite a bit," I said, "but I'm not exactly sure that it's my place to tell you."

"Well, you've already started, so there's no reason to stop now," Eloise said. It was more of an order than a question, and really, what could it hurt? She'd find out soon enough without me interfering.

At least that was what I was going to tell myself if anyone asked me about it later.

"Hank, I mean Henry, actually gave *her* the pub," I said.

"What do you mean, he gave it to her? Has he turned up?" she asked, the hope clear and heavy in her voice.

"No, at least not that I know of. Evidently Gregory never owned it, at least not officially. He held possession until some of your son's other assets could be liquidated. I'm not sure if it was a legal angle or if he just wanted to make things a little harder to uncover, but Sissy is at Gregory's office right now, signing the final paperwork. From what I understand, it will be hers sometime later today."

"Why would Henry even do that?" she asked herself softly before turning back to me. "What assets did he liquidate?"

"I have no idea," I admitted. "Maybe you should talk to Gregory."

"Maybe I should," she said. "I'm afraid this could mean trouble."

"That's what all of us were wondering, too," I said.

"All? Who else knows about it?" She looked quite surprised that I seemed to be more tuned into her small town's developments than she was.

"Let's see. Jake, Chief Vickers, Gregory, Sissy, and I were all standing in front of the Bridger house, talking, not all that long ago. Someone got in there again today, but you already know that, don't you?" I said.

"Yes, your husband told me. That was why I loaned him that car. That reminds me. I need to have the locks on those doors changed immediately. Excuse me for one second," Eloise said. She stepped away and made a quick phone call before returning to me. "I've got my man taking care of it this afternoon. The truth of the matter is that there have been far too many people coming and going there lately to suit my taste."

I could have kept my mouth shut right then and there, but I decided to admit why I'd been there in the first place. If she threw Jake and me out of her guesthouse because of my impertinence, then so be it, but I didn't want it on my conscience. "I was there taking photos of Shannon's room for a friend of mine back in April Springs. Someone clearly got there before I did, though. As a matter of fact, they were still there when I arrived."

"How could you tell? Did you see who it was?" She looked truly alarmed by the turn my story had taken.

I shook my head. "No, but the bed was pulled away from the wall, and a hiding place had been exposed."

"Was there anything inside it?" She looked really intent now.

"There wasn't a thing there," I admitted, "but that doesn't mean there wasn't earlier."

"What makes you suspect that someone was still there when you arrived?" she asked me.

"I tried to call Jake, but I couldn't get a signal inside the house, so I walked out back. I had him on the phone when I heard the front door slam, but by the time I got around the house, whoever had been there was already gone. It could have been your son, Eloise."

"Do you truly think it's possible that it was my Henry?" she asked me as she watched my expression.

"I honestly don't know, but I'd have to admit the thought did cross my mind," I acknowledged.

"Did your little group come up with any theories as to where my son might be if the intruder wasn't Henry?" she asked me pointedly. It clearly bothered her to have to ask me about it.

"A few possibilities were discussed," I admitted.

"Such as?"

I didn't really want to tell her, but honestly, what choice did I have? "We figured that he could be in hiding close by, but there's also the possibility that he went to Europe to find Shannon once and for all."

"Why on earth would he do that?"

"From what everyone has said, he never really got over her," I said. "It might explain why he liquidated some of his assets and put the pub in Sissy's name." I wasn't about to share the theory with her that Hank might have been robbed of his money before he could leave town. If that had happened, why hadn't he come home? One of the strongest possibilities was that he wasn't able to, that someone had killed him to cover up their crime. I couldn't bring myself to tell her that, no matter how hard she pushed me.

"Henry didn't leave town," she said after a few more moments of silence.

"How could you possibly know that?" I asked her.

"A mother knows that sort of thing," she said dismissively.

"I'm afraid everyone's going to need a little more proof than that," I answered. "Do you have anything more concrete than your motherly intuition?"

"Not at the moment, no," she said.

"I get it, Eloise. We all want your son to be here and safe. My husband and Chief Vickers are both doing everything in their power to find him."

"Then they'd better hurry," she said a bit ominously. "If they don't find my son soon, I'm afraid that something terrible is going to happen to him."

Why did everyone keep saying that? Was it possible that they knew more about the situation than Jake and I ever could, or were they just filled with dread over the prospect of the missing man being gone for good?

After my shower, I felt much better. The aroma of donuts, no matter how big a part of me it was, could get a little cloying at times, even

for me. I drove into town and looked for a place to eat. I was considering the diner where Jake had had his breakfast when a sign caught my
eye.

It was the Parsons Pond Pub, Sissy's new business. Eloise had rec-
ommended it, and my new friend now owned it.

Why not?

I looked at the menu and ordered a burger and fries along with a
soda, figuring that was a pretty safe set of choices. As I waited for my
order, I got up and walked around the place. The bar was prominent-
ly placed—no surprise there—and took up a third of the large room.
Still, that left plenty of space for tables and booths. The pub was dark,
filled with shades of ebony, and the light was a little sparse for my taste,
but no one else seemed to mind. The place was doing pretty good business. As I walked around the pub, I saw framed photos everywhere on
the walls. It was a nice touch, and it felt as though many of the lo-
cals had brought in their own pictures to make the place feel more like
home. Near the entrance, I saw a few faces that caught me by surprise.
Standing in front of a *Congratulations Graduates* sign were some of the
folks I'd recently met, though they were much younger in the photo.
All of them were dressed in their high school robes, and each was smiling brightly for the camera. I studied the names printed below the shot
and read, in order, "Bo, Shannon, Hank, and Gregory, The Four Mus-
keteers!" Bo had more hair and Gregory was thinner than he was now,
but it was the middle two recent grads that drew my attention. Hank
was handsome, well built, and looked as though he had the world by
the tail, but it was Shannon who really caught my eye. She was vivacious
even in the grainy old photograph, and her smile was practically lumi-
nescent. The girl was a real knockout, and everyone else seemed to lean
in toward her, as if she exuded some kind of power over them. Hank's
arm was tightly around her, but Bo had his arm around her as well. Gregory even managed to put a hand on Shannon's shoulder, as though
her touch was something magical. Shannon had one arm around Hank,

and the other hand was holding her diploma out for all of the world to see. She was the only one of the four showing proof that she'd just graduated, and I wondered if it was significant. The gown that would normally cover the arm that was holding the diploma was pulled up, and I saw a shadow on her wrist. I was studying the image and wishing it wasn't quite so grainy when a waitress approached me. "Your burger's ready," she said.

I nodded. "Thanks," I said as I followed her to my table.

It was every bit as good as Eloise had said it would be, and I was glad that I'd come. I couldn't wait to bring Jake back there, since he was a huge fan of burgers himself. As I ate the last bite, my cell phone rang, and when I glanced at the caller ID, I saw that it was my husband. "I just had the best burger I've had in ages, and that includes the ones they serve at the Boxcar Grill, though if you tell Trish I said that, I'll deny it until I'm blue in the face. Have you eaten yet?"

"No, and I won't be any time soon," he said. "Hank Sandler just showed up in Parson Pond."

"Have you talked to him?" I asked, desperate for information about the missing developer.

"No, we haven't actually seen him ourselves, but we got a tip that he was going into Mayor Humphries's house not three minutes ago. We're heading over there right now."

"Would it be okay if I met you there?" I asked as I put enough cash down to cover my bill and a nice tip as well.

"Why don't you let us check it out, and then I'll call you back," Jake said.

"Okay, I can do that," I said, a little disappointed that I wouldn't be on the scene.

"I'll be in touch," Jake said. Instead of hanging up, though, he quickly added, "Did you say that the house was on Hickory Street?"

"1284," the chief said in the background.

"That's what I thought," Jake said, and only then did he end the call.

It wasn't a direct invitation for me to join them, but the message was clear enough.

And if, by pure coincidence, I happened to be in the vicinity, I might just get to see what happened next myself.

At least Jake and Chief Vickers got there before I did. It might have been a little embarrassing if I'd been there waiting for them.

They were at the door as I parked and approached them. The chief looked at me with absolutely no surprise showing on his face. He must have known what Jake had done, and for all I knew, he might not have even minded. He had more on his plate than worrying about me at the moment, anyway.

"Chief, Jake, it's nice to see you. How did you know I'd be here?" the mayor asked as he opened his front door and stepped outside, closing it quickly behind him.

"You always go home for lunch, Hump," the chief said.

"I must be getting too predictable. Was there something I could help you with?"

"We're here to see Hank," Chief Vickers said.

The mayor paused just a beat too long before answering. "I don't know what you're talking about, fellas." He'd decided to go with trying to play it cool, but I didn't believe him, and I couldn't imagine that two seasoned law enforcement officers would be taken in, either.

"Mayor Humphries," Jake said evenly, "we know he just arrived. If he's in the house, you're obliged to produce him."

"What makes you think he's here?" Mayor Humphries asked them. If he noticed me in the background listening in, he didn't acknowledge it.

"We got a tip," Chief Vickers said.

"Let me guess; it was anonymous," the mayor said as he looked across the street. "Millie Wainwright has nothing better to do with her time than look out that big picture window all day. I'm getting tired of her jumping at shadows every time she feels a little isolated over there and decides to stir things up."

"Are you refusing to produce him?" the chief asked the mayor delicately.

"Even if I admitted that he was here, which I'm not, what right do you have to demand that I bring him out here to you? What crime has he committed?"

"Come on, Hump," the chief said cordially. "We all want the same thing. If he's here, let me talk to him. Half the town is worried sick about him."

"It's Mr. Mayor to you, Chief," the mayor said stiffly. "I don't know where Hank Sandler is at this moment, and that's the truth. Now if you'll excuse me, my lunch is getting cold." With that, he pivoted and walked back inside. He didn't exactly slam the door, but he didn't wave good-bye as he did so, either.

"He's lying," I said as I approached the men.

"Suzanne, what a surprise seeing you here," the chief said dryly. It was clear by his demeanor that he hadn't been surprised at all by my arrival.

"Why would he lie?" I asked, ignoring the jibe.

"We can't be sure that he didn't just tell us the truth," the chief said.

"Come on, Bo, we both know that he was lying through his teeth," Jake said. "Suzanne makes a good point. If the mayor knew where Hank was, or if the man was inside his house, why wouldn't he tell us?"

"I have no idea," the police chief said. "Come on, let's go talk to Millie."

As they walked across the street, I tagged along at a discreet pace. If Chief Vickers minded, he didn't say so. I took that as his tacit approval, though I stayed back far enough not to be intrusive.

It was clear that Millie Wainwright wasn't that surprised to see the parade head for her front door. She opened it before Jake and the chief could even ring her doorbell. Millie had to be in her nineties, but there was nothing about her that suggested her senses had dulled in the slightest over time. Her eyes were bright and her posture straight as she greeted the men. "So, you cracked the case as to who the anonymous tip came from, I see." There was an air of glee to her voice as she added, "It gives me faith in our police force knowing that a team of first-rate detectives is on the street, keeping us all safe."

"Millie, how sure are you that you just saw Hank Sandler go into the mayor's house?" Chief Vickers asked her.

"Bo, are you questioning my eyesight or my ability to identify a man I've known his entire life?" She was smiling as she asked it, but it was clear there was steel in her voice as well. This was not a woman to be trifled with.

"No, ma'am. I would never do that. I'm just following up."

"It was Hank, all right. He tried wearing one of those ridiculous hooded sweatshirts to disguise himself, but I would recognize that walk anywhere."

"You didn't see his face, though?" Jake asked her.

"You must be the intrepid state police inspector, which means that woman behind you is the famous donut maker," she said. She leaned forward and said, "I had one of your donuts this morning, young lady. You are an amazing chef."

"Thanks," I said, blushing a little from the attention.

Clearly Chief Vickers wasn't nearly as interested in my donut-making abilities. "Would you mind answering his question, Millie?"

She frowned for a moment before turning to the police chief. "No, I didn't see his face, but I knew it was him nonetheless. Are you going to arrest the mayor?"

"Why on earth would I do that?" Chief Vickers asked, clearly surprised by her question.

"He's harboring a fugitive," she said decisively.

"Hank isn't being accused of anything but disappearing," the chief explained. "There's no law against that."

"How about for obstructing an active police investigation? Surely someone's filed a missing-persons report with you by now."

"As a matter of fact, they haven't," the chief admitted.

"Then why are you here?"

"Our inquiry is a bit more informal than that," he admitted.

"What I'd like to know is who is paying *his* fee?" she asked him as she pointed to Jake.

"It was a private matter," the chief admitted reluctantly. Had Jake known that? If he had, he certainly hadn't shared that information with me.

"So Eloise pulled out her checkbook again, and everybody started hopping," Millie said a bit angrily. "Why am I surprised?" Inside, I heard a timer go off. It was faint, and I wasn't a hundred percent certain that the men had even noticed it, but a donut maker is tuned into these things. "Those would be my banana muffins," she said. "If you'll excuse me, I have *real* work that needs to be done."

She left us all standing outside as she closed the door and dismissed us.

"She identified him by his *walk*?" Jake asked the chief. "Does he have a distinctive limp or something?"

"Not that I've ever seen, and I've known Hank all my life," the chief said.

"What do you make of it then?" Jake asked him.

"Over the past nine months, Millie has reported prowlers in the neighborhood, a street gang of thugs roaming around after dark, and a cougar wandering the streets. Upon investigation, we found that the prowlers were men from a tree service leaving business cards in mailboxes, the street gang was a group of kids selling wrapping paper for school, and the cougar was Gretchen Barber's cat."

"So she's not exactly a reliable source," Jake said.

"Not exactly," he said.

"That still doesn't mean that the mayor isn't harboring Hank Sandler," I chimed in.

"It doesn't mean that he is, either," the chief said. "Come on, Jake. Let's go see if we can figure out our next step."

Jake shrugged in my direction and got into the squad car, but I wasn't quite ready to give up that easily yet.

"What?" the mayor asked as he opened his door to my summons. "Oh, it's you. I saw you lurking in the background, Suzanne. Was there something I could do for you?"

"I was wondering if you might have a minute," I said.

He looked impatiently at his watch, and as he did so, I tried to look inside to see if there was any evidence that Hank Sandler was or had recently been in the house.

I didn't see anything.

"Is there any chance you might spare a glass of water?" I asked. Surely the small-town mayor couldn't refuse such a simple request.

Instead of complying and letting me in, he reached inside, grabbed a cold bottle of water, and handed it to me. "I haven't even opened it yet. You can have this one."

I took the water, and as I did, he started to close the door. "Mr. Mayor, do you have Hank Sandler inside? Eloise and Sissy are really worried sick about him."

"He's not here," the mayor said, clearly losing patience with me.

"Maybe not this second, but was he here *earlier*?" I asked him, pushing a bit harder. After all, what did I have to lose? This wasn't April Springs, and I could afford to be a little more aggressive than I usually was back home.

"Good-bye, Suzanne," he answered, and then he closed the door.

I thought about walking around his house and peeking into his windows, but if I did that, either the mayor would catch me red-handed—an embarrassing enough situation—or Millie Wainwright would report that someone was trying to break into the mayor's house.

I still believed that the mayor had lied to us, despite his denial and Millie's questionable track record in reporting what she thought she saw.

How to prove it would be another matter entirely, though.

## Chapter 11

THERE REALLY WASN'T much else I could do at the moment as far as finding Hank Sandler was concerned, so I decided to walk around town and take in the sights. As I walked past shop after shop, my cell phone rang.

I brightened a little when I saw who was calling me. "Hi, Momma. How are you?"

"I'm fine, Suzanne. The question is how are you?"

"I couldn't be better," I said.

"Is Jake making any progress on the case?" she asked me. "Do you have any kind of time frame as to when you'll be coming back to April Springs?"

"You know how these things go. It's still early," I reminded her. It was a bit odd that she was checking up on me. "Momma, what's going on?"

"What do you mean?"

I glanced at my watch. "It's the heart of your afternoon, and I know how busy you are. There's got to be a reason you're taking time out to call me."

"Can't a mother just miss her daughter?" she asked me.

"She can, and I miss you too, but I can hear it in your voice. Something's going on."

She paused for a few moments, and then she admitted, "I'm worried about Gabby."

"What's up with Gabby?" I asked. "What has she gotten herself into this time?"

"It concerns this contractor of hers. What do you know about him?"

"Darrel Masters? Not a lot. We've chatted a few times. He seems a bit rough around the edges, but I can't speak to what kind of man he is.

Why do you ask?" I wasn't about to tell her that I thought Gabby and her contractor were getting to be more than that.

"Gabby seems to have gotten herself involved with him," Momma said.

"Well, he's rebuilding ReNEWed for her," I said, skirting the issue.

"Personally," Momma replied.

"I know all about it," I finally admitted. "I'm not sure it's such a good idea either, but why does it bother *you*? You have ties to the construction industry around April Springs. What have you been able to find out about him? Don't try to deny that you've already looked into him."

"That's the thing, Suzanne. This Masters fellow seems to have come out of the shadows. I can't find *anyone* who's ever worked with him before, and as far as public records are concerned, this is the first permit he's pulled in his life, at least in North Carolina."

That was troubling. "Is it possible that he worked for someone else before? Maybe he's starting out on his own, and Gabby's rebuild is his first project."

"I have Phillip digging into it," Momma said. "My husband is good at that sort of thing, but he's not as good as you and Jake are. The moment you get back, I'd like you to investigate this man's history and see what you can learn about him."

"You know I'd be happy to," I said, "but I can't make any promises as to when that might be."

"Has there been any sign of the man you're looking for?"

"The man *Jake* is looking for, you mean," I corrected her.

"I was most careful as to how I phrased the question. You can't tell me that you're not involved in the investigation as well as your husband."

"I might be on the perimeter of things," I reluctantly admitted. I hadn't kept her up to date on what had been happening on purpose. After all, what point would it serve but to make her worry about her daughter's safety? I'd learned as a teenager that there were some things in my life my mother didn't have to know about, and usually what she didn't know couldn't hurt her or me. I might have pushed that logic a little too far a time or two in the past, but I'd survived it, and so had she.

"Is there no sign of him? Perhaps he's just gone."

"Maybe, but the mayor here was spotted with him this morning by a neighbor. My guess is that Hank Sandler is hiding from someone or something."

"My, you do seem to get yourself embroiled in messes, don't you?" Momma asked.

As she spoke, I noticed Harley approaching, and by the glum expression on his face, he was not having a very good afternoon. "Momma, I need to go. I'll keep you posted."

"Be careful, Suzanne."

"I always am," I said, and then I put my phone away. "Harley, what's up?"

The retired police chief seemed surprised to find me standing in front of him, as though I'd materialized out of thin air. "Suzanne? Hi. What are you doing here?"

"Taking in the sights of your lovely little town," I said, trying to be more cheerful than I actually was feeling. In a softer voice, I asked, "Harley, are you okay?"

"Sure. Couldn't be better," he said, clearly lying but just as obviously not wanting to talk about it. Okay, I could respect that, at least for the moment.

"I'm glad I ran into you. I have a question you might be able to answer."

He nodded. "I'm kind of in your debt, so fire away."

I put my hands up in the air. "Hang on a second. I didn't pitch in at the donut shop this morning to curry favor with you or to make you beholden to me either. Forget I asked. I hope you have a nice afternoon. Good-bye."

I got three steps away from him when he caught up with me. "Suzanne, I'm sorry. That was rude of me. I know you didn't help me as some kind of quid pro quo. The truth is that I'm in a lousy mood, and I took it out on you. What do you want to know?"

"Are you sure?"

"As sure as I can be," he said with a grin.

"Fine. Do you know anything about Mayor Humphries's relationship with Hank Sandler?"

He looked at me carefully before he answered. "Why do you ask?"

I could keep it from him, but there was really no reason to. "An eyewitness spotted Hank going into the mayor's house not half an hour ago."

"Really? That's interesting." He paused a moment before asking, "It wasn't Millie Wainwright, was it? Of course it was. She lives right across the street from the Humphries house."

"Is she really that unreliable an eyewitness?" I asked him.

"You have no idea."

"Okay, but even if that's true, is there a chance she's right this time?" I asked him.

"That's always a possibility."

"Would Hank have a reason to be visiting the mayor when he's presumed missing?" I asked him.

"If you would have asked me that six months ago, I would have said no, but since then, they've gotten awfully chummy. Hump wasn't all that close to Hank for a great many years, but lately, they've been doing business together in real estate near the coast. Hump inherited some money from his grandfather, and Hank's been helping him find some rentals on the coast to invest in. From what I heard through the local grapevine, Hump was about to put the largest chunk of his newfound wealth into a place when Hank got wind of it. Evidently it was some kind of scam, and Hank saved the mayor's tail. He owes him big-time, and maybe Hank's cashing in the favor by getting Hump's help now. If he is, I'm sure Anna doesn't know about it. She's not Hank's biggest fan by any means. In fact, she's been openly hostile to him for more than a decade."

"Really? That long?" I asked. "What caused the rift between them?"

"Oh, that's right. I keep forgetting that you're not from around here. Anna always blamed Hank for Shannon leaving town. She's her niece, you know, and she still hasn't gotten over it."

"No, I didn't know," I said.

Harley just shrugged. "You know how it is in small towns. Just about everybody has ties to everybody else here one way or another. I'm sure April Springs is the same way."

"Sometimes it feels that way," I said. "So if you were a betting man, would you say that Hank is hiding out around here, or has something darker happened to him?"

Harley cocked his head and paused. "I've been thinking about it, and before I ran into you, I would have said that it was a coin flip, but now I'm not so sure. I'd have to say that there's a good chance that Hank is alive and well, though why he's hiding is beyond me."

"I have no idea, either," I admitted.

"You really take an interest in your husband's work, don't you?" Harley asked me a bit forlornly.

I wasn't about to admit that I'd been known to investigate police cases myself. "I try my best," I said.

"That must be really nice for him," Harley acknowledged.

"It is, but then again, Jake has never made a donut in his life unless it was under duress," I said, trying to cheer him up.

"You're just trying to make me feel better," he said.

"Guilty as charged, though it shouldn't be a crime. Harley, I know that we just met this morning, but sometimes talking to a stranger is easier than talking to an old friend. I'm a good listener, and I'm here for you."

He stared down at his shoes for a few moments, and then he finally said, "I'm starting to believe that the rumors about Delia and Hank aren't completely unfounded."

"I'm so sorry," I said as I touched his arm lightly. "Did something happen to change your mind?"

"You suggested that I didn't have to keep my shop open as long as I'd been doing, so I went home early to surprise my wife. I surprised her, all right."

"Was Hank there?" I asked.

"No, but she was on the phone with someone, and when she saw me walk into the kitchen, she tried to get off so fast she dropped her phone. I heard a man on the other end saying, 'Hello? Are you still there?' before she could hang up."

"Did you recognize the man's voice?" I asked.

"I couldn't swear to it, but it could have been Hank Sandler," he admitted.

"It might not have been him, though," I said, doing my best to offer him some kind of comfort. Max had cheated on me in our marriage, and I knew just how much it hurt. I decided to tell him my story, as painful as it was for me to recount. "My ex-husband had an affair with a woman in town while we were married, and it nearly broke me. I know you've heard whispers about Delia and Hank, but couldn't it have been someone else on the other end of that call?"

"Is that really any better? What does it matter if she's been seeing Hank or someone else entirely? Cheating is cheating."

"That's true enough, but is there even the slightest chance that it could have all been innocent?"

"Not judging by her expression when she saw me come in. She's up to something, Suzanne. I was a cop too long not to know it in my bones. The question is, what do I do about it? Do I turn a blind eye and hope she gets bored with whoever it is, or do I confront her and make a clean break of it? I've been trying to bury my head in the sand too long, hoping that it would all go away, but I'm not sure that I've got the stomach for that anymore. What did you do?"

"I'm not sure knowing would help you make up your mind, Harley. You have to remember that every marriage is different," I said.

"I know that, but I would also like to hear your story."

I owed the man the truth. He'd asked me for honesty, and that was what he was going to get, no matter how painful it might be for me to tell or for him to hear. "I divorced Max the second I found out. In fact, the moment I got my divorce settlement, I opened Donut Hearts and moved back in with my mother. It was about as clean a break as I could make without leaving town altogether, and I wasn't going to let him drive me out of the only place that had ever felt like home to me. Harley, it wasn't easy, but I was a better person for it when all was said and done. I learned to stand on my own two feet and to appreciate the fact that it wasn't my fault. That opened my heart enough for Jake to come in, and I can honestly say that I've never been happier in my life."

I suddenly realized that it seemed as though I was encouraging him to leave his wife, and I certainly didn't want that on my conscience. It was his decision, and his alone, to make. "But like I said, every situation is different. Some folks seem to be able to get past stormy weather in their marriages and are stronger because of it."

"Maybe some folks, but not me," he said glumly. "Thanks for the talk. You've helped me clarify my thinking."

I couldn't let him go like that. "Harley, don't do anything rash until you have the facts. I caught Max and his mistress red-handed. There was no doubt about what was going on, but from what you've told me, all you know for sure is that folks are talking about Delia and Hank. There might not be anything to it."

"I was a cop too long not to know that usually where there's smoke, a fire is burning nearby, usually out of control," he said.

"Still, don't you owe it to yourself to be sure of the truth before you do anything so permanent? If you're really thinking about leaving her, you need to be dead certain that there's a real reason for you to go. Come on, you were a cop. Would you ever accept the kind of evidence you've got so far on a case you were working on, or would you dig in and find out what the truth really was? It might not be easy to handle what you find out, but at least you'll know one way or the other."

"You're right," he said a bit grimly. "I need to know the truth, no matter what consequences it might bring."

"Remember, if I can help you, all you have to do is ask," I said, touching his shoulder lightly again. It was all I could do to help a fellow donut maker in trouble, at least until he asked me for more help directly. Otherwise, all I could do was be there for him and offer what support I could.

"You've already done more than any of my friends around here have done," he said, offering me a brave smile.

"Don't be too hard on them. After all, it's not easy giving hard advice," I countered.

"And yet you didn't seem to have any problem with it just now," he answered with the hint of a smile.

"Like I said, sometimes it's easier to talk to a stranger, and that goes both ways. Good luck, Harley."

"I appreciate that, but I'm not going to rely on luck. I'm going to dust off my old skill set and root out the truth, come what may."

"That's the spirit," I said.

I watched him walk away, and I realized that his step was firmer and his back was straighter than it had been since I'd met the man. I'd meant every word that I'd said to him. Knowing was better than not knowing, and he could deal with the truth once he was able to figure out exactly what that was. After all, he was taking the first step to figuring out the rest of his life. If Delia had indeed cheated on him, Harley could deal with that however he saw fit, and if it turned out that it had all just been in everyone else's imagination, he could accept that and get on with his marriage. At least if he knew what had really happened, he could get out of the rut of despair he seemed to be in at the moment.

Then again, maybe I'd butted into a man's life uninvited and ruined it. There were consequences to our actions that we couldn't always foresee, but he'd asked me for my advice, and I hadn't felt as though I could refuse it. What he did with what I'd told him was ultimately up to him.

That still didn't help me feel better.

Maybe I should have kept my mouth shut after all.

If that were true, it was too late to take anything back that I'd told him.

What happened next was entirely up to Harley.

## Chapter 12

MY TALK WITH HARLEY upset me so much that I didn't really want to be around people, so I headed back to the A-frame guest cottage so I could be alone. As nice as the place was though, I got a little stir crazy pretty quickly, so I decided to take a walk around the grounds. Eloise Sandler had a great deal of property around her home, and there were walking trails spread throughout it. I decided what I really needed was a good walk to clear my head, so I took off to enjoy the rest of the afternoon until I met up with Jake again.

The paths curved through thick woods, and it was difficult to know what was just a few steps ahead of me on the trail. Whoever had designed the particular walkway I was on had clearly used a snake's back as a straight edge. As I neared one hairpin section, I heard an angry voice coming from the other side of a thick stand of bamboo.

It was our host, Eloise Sandler.

"I don't care. This is ridiculous. You need to act your age and do the right thing. Stop behaving like a child! What? Hello? You did not just hang up on me!"

It sounded as though she'd been talking to one of her children, but which one, Sissy or Hank?

I made my way around the bamboo and found her sitting on a bench in front of a long, narrow pool of water that was close to her house. I hadn't even realized where I'd been heading. That explained the bamboo. It had been designed as some sort of meditation area, and I could see an arched bridge over the water and lilies beneath it. It truly was an amazing spot, full of tranquility and serenity, but there was none of either trait on my hostess's face.

"Eloise, are you okay?"

She visibly jumped at the sound of my voice. "Suzanne! What are you doing here?"

"I thought I'd take a walk. I hope that's okay," I said apologetically.

"Of course, it's fine," she said, quickly composing herself.

"Was that Henry on the phone just now?" I asked her.

"What? No. Of course not. I don't know where my son is!" She was protesting an awful lot, and I had to wonder if I'd guessed right.

"Then it was Sissy?" I followed up.

"Do you have children, Suzanne?" she asked me, ignoring my direct question.

"No, not yet," I said.

"Well, they are truly an equal mix of blessing and burden," she answered.

"I can imagine," I replied, trying to sound as sympathetic as I could.

She sat there shaking her head slightly, and then she suddenly stood. "If only that were true. I'd love to stay and chat, but I have a meeting soon. Enjoy your stroll."

"Thanks," I said to her retreating back as she walked the three dozen feet back to her door.

Something had changed in her. Eloise had gone from a worried woman to a frustrated one, and I had to believe that she'd just been talking to her son despite her denials. What was the right thing she was urging him to do? Come forward, or was it something more significant than that? I'd pressed her as hard as I could, but I needed to tell Jake what I'd just overheard.

It could change everything.

"Can you talk?" I asked as he picked up my call.

"For a minute. Bo got a phone call himself, and he stepped outside to take it. He doesn't look happy, whoever he's talking to," Jake said with a hint of amusement in his voice.

"There must be a lot of that going around," I said.

There was a moment of pause on the other end before he answered. "Yeah, I think so, too. Something's going on, Suzanne, but I'm not quite sure what it is."

"Are we staying in Parsons Pond?" I asked.

He sounded surprised by my question. "Of course we are. Why wouldn't we?"

"Well, I just figured that since it seems as though Hank Sandler is alive and well, your job is finished here."

"I was hired to *find* him, and I haven't done that yet. As long as they want me, I'm sticking to this. What's going on? Are you ready to go home?"

"Not without you I'm not," I said firmly. "Is there any chance we could have dinner together tonight, or are things too crazy for you?"

"I'm not sure. Can I get back to you on that?"

"Of course. I'm going to be at the guesthouse the rest of the afternoon. As a matter of fact, I might even take a nap."

"That's what I would do if I had the choice," he answered with a laugh. "Gotta go. Bo's coming back, and he doesn't look happy. I'm guessing he's having more trouble with his sister."

"Bye," I said to dead air.

I had to wonder what was going on with Ginny. Did she suspect that Hank was in town, too? I couldn't imagine the police chief being very happy with his sister if she had decided to give the man another chance. Then again, it might have been someone else entirely. Was there any chance that Eloise had called him after leaving me? Probably not. At the dinner party the night before, she hadn't exactly shown that she had a lot of confidence in him or his abilities. If she had, she never would have called Jake in on the case. At least Hank Sandler was alive. I felt confident in believing that, though I wasn't sure how long that might stay true. What had he gotten himself into that he felt forced to hide from the folks who cared about him? Whatever it was, I didn't think it was insignificant.

Hopefully Jake and the police chief would be able to smoke him out. Once they did, our part of this would be over and we could go back home. I'd met some nice people in Parsons Pond, but they all had their own sets of problems, and the more I got to know them, the more I became involved in their lives. I had enough of that back in April Springs. I'd come with Jake to get some kind of vacation, and instead, I'd ended up working in a donut shop and snooping into other people's lives.

It truthfully wasn't all that much of a vacation from my usual life.

Yes, a nap sounded better by the minute as I made my way back to the A-frame. I settled onto the couch, turned on the gas fireplace, and stretched out on the couch.

If I couldn't nod off in those circumstances, there was no hope for me at all.

I was awakened by the sound of someone unlocking the front door, and I bolted upright. Was someone breaking into the guest cottage?

"Sorry, I didn't mean to wake you," Jake said with a grin as he walked over and kissed me. "Have a nice nap?"

"Not really. I was being chased around the barn by cartoon cows," I said as I rubbed my eyes. "It wasn't the most restful sleep I've ever had in my life." I glanced at the clock. "You're back sooner than I expected."

"Our leads dried up, and Chief Vickers decided to stop early. Something's going on with Ginny, but he wouldn't tell me anything more than that," he said. "If you're up for it, I thought we might have dinner at The Branch Inn."

"Oh, I heard about that. It's what passes for fine dining around here. That sounds great to me."

"Good. How much time do you need to get ready?" he asked.

"Seven minutes should be enough," I answered.

He smiled as he pretended to push a button on his watch. "Ready. Set. Go."

I beat my projected time by ninety seconds, and we were on our way to dinner and hopefully a little quality time alone afterward.

That sounded like an excellent vacation to me.

"So, how goes the investigation?" I asked Jake as he drove us to the inn's restaurant. "Is there anything you can talk about?"

"There's really not much to tell," he said. "There hasn't been *any* activity on Hank Sandler's credit cards or his cell phone in the last twenty-four hours, two pretty big red flags as far as I'm concerned. In this day and age, it's hard to imagine someone going for very long without either one."

"He's not dead, Jake," I said.

"It would be nice to believe that, but we can't go on one unreliable eyewitness and a hunch. You need to at least consider the possibility that he's dead, Suzanne."

"Maybe, but let me tell you what I think," I said. "I heard Eloise talking to someone on the phone this afternoon, and I'm willing to put money on the fact that it was her son."

That got his attention. "Did she call him by name?"

"No, but she did everything *but* say Henry."

"What exactly did you hear?" he asked me.

I thought back to the conversation. "She said that it was ridiculous, that whoever was on the other end needed to act their age, do the right thing, and stop acting like a child."

"You're right. That sounds *exactly* like something a mother would say to her child," Jake agreed. "She could have been talking to Sissy, though."

"Maybe, but I don't think so," I insisted.

"Based on what exactly?"

"My gut," I replied, not having a more satisfying answer. "Don't discount my hunches, Jake. We both know that in the past, I've been..."

"Slow down, Suzanne. You don't have to convince me that your instincts are often right. If we go on the assumption that Hank Sandler really is still alive, then he's staying with someone in town, and he's got plenty of cash, or whoever is harboring him does."

"Doesn't the mayor fit under both of those conditions?" I asked him.

"Maybe, but why would he put his neck on the line like that? It's pretty clear that Eloise Sandler runs this town, and he's probably serving as mayor depending on her good graces."

"Oh, that's right. I haven't told you about that yet either."

Jake pulled the truck over well before we arrived at the restaurant. "What haven't you told me?"

"I had a chat with the former police chief and current donut maker for Parsons Pond," I said.

"And what exactly did you two talk about?"

I wasn't about to tell my husband that I'd been giving the man marital advice. "This and that, but it came up in our conversation that Hank kept the mayor from losing a great deal of money recently, and Hump is in his debt in a big way."

"Then maybe Hank was there after all, and Millie Wainwright wasn't wrong."

"Maybe, but there's a hiccup to that theory," I told him.

"Like what?"

"Anna, the mayor's wife, was Shannon Bridger's aunt, and she still blames Hank for Shannon leaving town so abruptly. Evidently the woman holds a grudge, so the mayor would have to sneak around if he was going to harbor Hank Sandler, especially without his wife's knowledge or, more importantly, her approval."

"Still, there could be something there. The issue is that the mayor was right about what he said earlier. There hasn't even been a missing-persons report filed on Hank Sandler yet, so all of our inquiries have been unofficial so far."

"So in actuality, you don't have any more right to investigate this case than I do."

"Are you investigating?" he asked me. "Forget it. I don't want to know."

I kissed his cheek and smiled. "That's one of the many things I love about you. You don't usually ask me a question you don't want to know the answer to."

"Fine. What else do you know?" he asked me.

"Unofficially? You're not going to share this with the police chief, are you? I've got a hunch he wouldn't like me digging into this."

"Are you kidding? He's not happy that *I'm* around," Jake said. "The man's got a bit of a temper. He hides it well, but it's there nonetheless. I think he feels as though he has something to prove after taking over for Harley. I'm not saying that there's any bad blood between them per se, but I don't think either man is the president of the other one's fan club. My guess is that Bo Vickers wants all of the credit for tracking down Hank himself. If I didn't know better, I'd think that he was withholding information from me."

"Why do you say that?"

"That phone conversation he had earlier while you and I were chatting on the phone, for one thing. He was visibly upset after it, but when I pressed him about it, he brushed it off."

"It must be tough for him having Harley around," I said. "From what I can tell, just about everybody loves the man."

"Just about?" he asked me.

I thought about telling him about Delia, but I wasn't sure it was my business. After all, Harley had talked to me in confidence, and while I knew Jake wouldn't spread it around, I wasn't sure he needed to know. And then I realized that maybe he did. "Okay, it's important to remember that what I'm about to tell you was told to me in strictest confidence."

"I won't breathe a word of it if I can help it," Jake said. "You can trust me."

"I know that. I just feel bad sharing Harley's secret with anyone else."

"Then don't tell me," Jake said calmly.

It was one of the few things my husband did that frustrated me. "The only problem with that is that it might be relevant to the case you're working on."

He sat there in silence for several moments before he said, "I can't be the judge of whether it is important or not. That has to be your decision, Suzanne, and I respect you enough to know that you'll make the right one."

So the ball was thoroughly in my court. "Fine. There's a rumor going around that Delia and Hank have been having an affair."

Jake nodded. "I got wind of that earlier. There isn't much to back it up though, is there?"

"Harley isn't so sure about that," I admitted.

Jake whistled. "So, if Delia's been cheating on her husband with Hank and he threatened to expose her, Hank might have forced her into helping him."

"That doesn't put him in a very good light, does it?"

"Suzanne, if he's having an affair with a married woman, doesn't that give us the right to judge him by his behavior at least a *little* bit?"

"Maybe. You know how I feel about infidelity, but I've got to remind you that they are just rumors at this point."

"Then Harley needs to figure out if they are based on fact or not," Jake said.

"That's exactly what I told him this afternoon," I answered softly. I looked over at Jake, but he didn't react to the news that I'd been meddling in other people's lives again. "Aren't you going to say something?"

"There's nothing for me to say," he answered.

"Come on. You've got to say *something*," I prodded him.

"Dear sweet wife, you were trying to help the man. I get it. No one should fault you for wanting the best for your friends."

"I just met him today," I said.

"Maybe so, but it sounds as though you two are simpatico. I trust you in those situations to read the mood correctly and do the right thing."

I had hoped for something from him that I could react to, but instead, he'd been calm and even rational in his response. That left me only one choice.

I had to answer in kind. "The truth is that I'm not a hundred percent sure that I did the right thing after all," I admitted. "Maybe I should have kept my nose out of his business."

"That's not really in your nature though, is it? Don't get me wrong; it's one of the things I love most about you. I'm sure you didn't say anything to the man that he wasn't already wondering about himself."

"Probably, but it still makes me wonder if I chose the right path."

"You'll go crazy asking yourself that kind of question," Jake said as he started the truck and pulled back out onto the road. "Let's get something to eat. I'm starving."

"I am, too," I admitted. "Did you have lunch?"

"If you could call it that," he admitted. "The chief has pretty pedestrian tastes. I love a good sandwich as much as the next guy, but it needs to be a good one, you know? We ate in some dive two towns away that used some questionable meat if you ask me."

"You should try the pub," I told him. "Their burgers are amazing."

"Did you happen to see Sissy or Gregory there?" he asked me. "Maybe even have time for an informal questioning session or two while you were eating?"

"As a matter of fact, neither one of them was there, but I did see an interesting photo on the wall of Bo, Shannon, Hank, and Gregory on the day of their graduation from high school."

"Did you take a picture of it with your cell phone?" Jake asked me. "I'd love to see it."

"No, I didn't even think about it. Should I have taken one?"

"I was just curious," he said.

"Tell you what, when I have lunch there tomorrow, I'll take a picture for you then," I promised him. "Care to join me?"

"I wish I could, but we'll probably be eating out of the back of some food truck off the highway again," he said wistfully. "That's why I want to make tonight count."

"*Any* meal I share with you counts," I said with a grin.

"I agree, but you have to admit that a steak is better than cheese and crackers," he said as he pulled into the crowded parking lot.

"That would depend on the cheese and crackers, the quality of the steak, and who you eat the meal with," I answered him.

"That it would," he said. "Come on. Let's go see just how good this place really is."

## Chapter 13

"EXCUSE ME," MAYOR HUMPHRIES said absently as he nearly ran into us on our way into the restaurant. His wife, Anna, was in tow, and the two of them seemed as though they couldn't wait to get out of the building.

"Mr. Mayor, why the rush?" I asked him.

"Oh, it's the Harts. Or the Bishops, I should say," he corrected himself quickly.

"Seen any old friends lately?" I asked him coyly.

His wife seemed puzzled by the question, but the mayor was clearly disturbed by my reference to Hank, and after talking to Harley, I knew why. If Anna knew that her husband was helping Hank, she wouldn't be happy about it, and I wondered if that might have had something to do with their abrupt exit.

"I see old friends every day," he said. "Now if you'll excuse us, we need to go."

Anna didn't seem willing to budge though. "I've never seen you brush someone off in your life, Hiram Humphries! What's going on?"

His first name was Hiram? No wonder he went by Hump. "I explained it all to you before, dear. We need to get home. I believe I left the front door unlocked."

"As if that would matter in Parsons Pond," she said with a frown.

"Besides, these folks—as nice as they are—aren't voters here."

"That's still no excuse to be rude to them. They are guests of Eloise Sandler, and I expect you to act better toward them."

So it was our status of being linked to Eloise that mattered to her. It was odd given the way she felt about the woman's son, but then again, I knew from firsthand experience that small towns could form some odd alliances and even stranger enemies.

"Forgive us, but we really do have to run," he said as he glanced back into the restaurant briefly. Was he trying to get away from someone inside? I was going to have to make it a point to look around the place. "Come, Anna."

"Oh, very well." Almost as an aside, she added, "You're not fooling me, you know."

"What are you talking about?" he asked her, and when I glanced at his face I saw that his complexion had gone white.

"I saw Buford Cummings at the bar. You really do hate that man, don't you?"

"He punched me in the nose," the mayor said vehemently.

"You were in the fifth grade! Get over it," she scolded him as they walked out.

So much for the mystery of their sudden departure.

We were seated at a table near the bathrooms, which wasn't an ideal location, but it did give us a chance to survey the room. Besides, it was the only table they had available, even though we were there early, at least for most people. It might have been later for me, but my normal work schedule dictated that we eat before most folks did. Apparently that was more of a habit here than it was back in April Springs. In fact, I hadn't seen a restaurant that crowded so close to five in a long time.

"This is nice," I said after the waiter took our orders, a promised steak and potato for Jake and salmon for me.

"Yes, it is," Jake said, clearly distracted by something.

"Convenient, too," I added.

"Yes."

"I mean if you have a sudden need of the facilities, right there they are, only steps away," I commented.

"Handy," Jake answered as he stared at his fingers.

"Okay, buster, what's going on with you? I'm your wife, not a potted plant. When my husband takes me out to dinner, I expect to get just a little bit of his attention."

He looked up at me and frowned. "Sorry. I was a little bit lost for a minute there."

"What's going on, Jake?" I asked him softly. "Is something wrong?"

"Suzanne, what are we doing here? I've been thinking about what you said earlier, and I'm starting to believe that you were right."

"Of course I was. What exactly was I right about in particular this time?"

"Hank is clearly alive and well, so it doesn't seem all that vital that we hang around so I can stay and help find him. I feel like I'm spinning my wheels. The mayor *and* our hostess are probably both lying to us, and I'm pretty sure that my partner in the investigation is holding out on me, too. I feel about as useless as a refrigerator salesman at the North Pole. Should we pack it in and head home tomorrow?"

"Jake, it's not like you to be willing to give up like this," I said as I patted his hand. "We *suspect* that Hank is alive, but is he really well? I don't think this is some kind of game. Something stinks in Parsons Pond, and you need to figure out what it is. I've got a bad feeling about this case, that things are going to get worse before they get better. If you don't find Hank, and I mean fast, he might not be alive for much longer."

My husband looked at me oddly. "Why do you think that?"

"It feels like the tension around here is quickly building to its boiling point," I said as I looked up and saw Ginny Vickers, the police chief's sister, heading toward us. Well, it wasn't exactly toward us. She was going to the restroom, but she at least tried to smile and nod in our direction on her way, though it was pretty clear that she was about to burst out crying.

"Should I go see if she's okay?" I asked him after she hurried past us.

He was about to answer when Chief Vickers approached. "Hello, Suzanne. Jake, good to see you."

"Hello, Chief," Jake said.

"Is your sister okay, Bo?" I asked him.

"No, I'm afraid she's not," he admitted.

"Should I go check on her?" I offered.

"Let's give her a few minutes. Maybe she can cry it out. If you go in, she'll think I sent you, and that's just going to make matters worse. May I?" he asked as he sat down without waiting for a formal invitation.

"Of course," my husband said graciously after the fact.

"Jake, I owe you an apology," the chief said as he looked Jake directly in the eye.

"For what exactly?" he asked the police chief.

"I've been a pretty sad excuse for a partner ever since you showed up, but the truth is that I've had a lot on my mind. When Hank broke Ginny's heart, it nearly destroyed her. I warned him not to date her unless he was serious, but he promised me that he wouldn't hurt her. She's had a crush on him since we were all kids. I'm not sure when Hank noticed her, but a few months ago, he asked her out, and of course she jumped at the chance. I'd heard stories about Hank fooling around, and I tried to warn Ginny, but she wouldn't listen. I don't know why I was even surprised. He's been that way since we all left high school, but I sure hate seeing my little sister like this."

I hadn't exactly warmed all that much to the chief before, but I could see the pain in his eyes now, and I felt sorry for him.

I made an executive decision and stood up. "I'm going to go check on her."

"I'm not sure..." the chief said.

"It's my call, Chief," I answered.

"Ginny, are you okay?" I asked the woman behind the closed bathroom stall door. I could hear her softly weeping on the other side. It broke my heart, and we weren't even related. No wonder the chief had been out of sorts. It had to be doubly hard that he had been pressed into finding his old friend after what he'd so recently done to his sister.

"I'm fine," she said, and then she blew her nose and came out. "I'm sorry you had to see me like this, Suzanne."

"Don't apologize. Do you want to try splashing some cold water on your face? I wish I had some eye drops." Her eyes were blazing red, a sure sign that she'd been crying.

"I carry around liquid tears these days," she said, trying her best to smile. "Did Bo send you in here?"

"No. As a matter of fact, I came against his advice," I admitted, which happened to be true. "He did tell us about you and Hank and that he was worried that it might turn out this way."

"That's my big brother, always looking out for me," she said as she sniffed a few times. "He warned me, but I wouldn't listen. I'd heard the rumors about Hank, but I refused to believe them. I've got to give Bo credit. He hasn't once said that he told me so, even though he had every right to. Why didn't I listen to him?"

I touched her shoulder lightly. "Hey, don't be so hard on yourself. Love can be a tough thing to deal with sometimes."

"Don't I know it," she said. "You seem happy with your husband."

"I am, but there's something you should know. Jake is my *second* husband," I admitted.

"Really? I had no idea."

"How could you?" I asked. "It's been my experience that old crushes are usually the hardest ones to get over. Trust me on that."

"It might not have been so bad if he'd just lost interest in me over time, but it was so sudden! It was almost as though he couldn't stand to be in the same room with me anymore. Thank goodness I'd moved back in with Bo when I lost my job! He's been there for me every second since."

"He sounds like a good brother to have on your side," I said as she put drops in each eye.

"When all of his friends went off to college after high school, he joined the Army, and I thought I'd lost him forever, but he came back and joined the police force here four years later after our folks died. Something about the military changed him, and it took us years to get reacquainted. I'm not sure what happened to him when he served, and he's never really talked about it, but I'm guessing it was bad. Anyway, things were finally getting good between us again when Hank dumped me." She looked in the mirror, did some basic makeup repair, and then turned to me. "I'm afraid that's as good as I'm going to get."

"I think you look perfect," I told her. "I know it doesn't feel that way right now, but hearts do find a way of healing."

"I know. I just wish it wouldn't take so long."

"I know exactly what you mean," I said with a smile. "Shall we go back out and face the world again?"

"Why not? My food's probably cold by now, anyway."

"If that's as bad as it gets, life's still pretty good," I reminded her.

"Don't I know it," she said. Ginny squeezed my hand. "Thanks for rescuing me."

"Thank your brother," I said.

"So he did send you in," she countered.

"No, I did that on my own, but you told me yourself that he's been there for you through this, and I'm sure he'll see it through to the end with you. Family's important," I said, thinking of mine.

"I think so, too," she said. "With Mom and Dad gone, we're all we've got left now."

"It's enough," I told her.

When we rejoined Bo and Jake at the table, the police chief looked expectantly at his sister. "Is everything okay, Sis?"

"Sorry about that," Ginny said quickly as she put on a brave smile. "I'm afraid our food is cold by now."

"I had them take it back into the kitchen and keep it warm for us," Bo admitted. "We can get it to go and take it back home if you'd rather eat there."

"No, I think I'm ready to be seen in public again," Ginny said. She leaned over and told Jake, "You've got yourself a good one there, sir."

"I think so, too," Jake said with a smile.

"See you in the morning," the chief told my husband.

"Sounds good."

After they returned to their table, Jake said, "He's not such a bad guy after all. He clearly loves his sister."

"The feeling's mutual. It just goes to show you, doesn't it?"

"What's that?"

"People are often more than one thing."

"I'm not sure that sentence is strictly grammatically correct," my husband said with a grin, "but I agree with the sentiment."

"Well, since neither one of us is a high school English teacher, I think we'll be fine."

Our food soon arrived, and it was every bit as good as promised.

As Jake collected his change from the bill and left our waiter a healthy tip, he told me, "For a small town, this area has some good food."

"And you haven't even eaten at the pub yet," I told him.

"No, but I'm going to make it a point to before we leave Parsons Pond," Jake said.

"I don't blame you," I said as we walked out into the parking lot only to discover two other people we knew having a rather heated argument.

I had been right earlier.

This town was a powder keg just waiting to explode, and this was just one more example of it.

## Chapter 14

"SISSY, HOW MANY TIMES do I have to tell you? It's simply not true!" Gregory Kline said loudly to Sissy Sandler as she stood by her car. The two of them had parked side by side, and Sissy had her hand on the handle of her driver's-side door.

"You can keep saying that until you're blue in the face, but I'll *never* believe you. I *know* I'll never be good enough for you, at least as far as you're concerned. Shannon's been gone fourteen years, Gregory, and yet you and Hank both act as though she left yesterday!"

The attorney, obviously fighting to keep his voice calm, said, "You asked me why I thought Hank took off, and I told you. Did I have a crush on her? Of course I did! So did Billy Winston, Larry Jansen, Bo Vickers, and Steve Barrister! For all I know, Mr. Cruickshank, the PE teacher, had one on her, too. She was just that kind of girl, but I got over it, even if your brother never did!"

"That's because she would never go out with *you*!" Sissy said.

"It was just a stupid crush," he said a little more softly.

"Like the one I used to have on *you*?" Sissy asked him.

"Come on, be fair," Gregory said, now pleading with her.

"No. I thought it might work, but now I can see that it's not going to. Good night, and good-bye, Gregory."

"Sissy, don't go," he begged.

Her only answer was to get into her car and drive off. I had a feeling that if Gregory hadn't stepped out of her way at the last second, Sissy might have clipped him. She was in that big a hurry to get away from him, and I could see that she was crying as she drove off.

"I don't believe it," Gregory said more to himself than to us. In fact, if he knew we were even there, he didn't show it. "Shannon's been gone all this time and she's *still* screwing up my life!"

"Are you okay?" Jake asked him as we approached.

The attorney looked startled and not at all happy to see us standing there. "I suppose you heard all of that humiliating experience."

"Dating isn't easy," I said.

"Especially when there are three of you in the picture," he said. "I swear to all that's holy and good that I got over Shannon Bridger years ago. Did I want her, too? Of course I did! Every guy in school wanted to be with her, but she wanted Hank and just Hank! She made that clear enough to the rest of us! What he did to run her off I'll never know, but it ruined quite a few friendships when she left here so abruptly. Hank and I were never the same, and even Bo held it against him, and he wanted to be like Hank more than anything in the world. I went off to a different school and Bo went into the Army, something he *never* would have done if she hadn't walked out on us all."

"It tore you up too, didn't it?" Jake asked him.

"For a while, but then I started getting angry with her. If she would have walked back into my life and asked me for a fresh start any time in the past ten years, I would have turned her down cold. You just don't do that to people you care about."

"I didn't know you and Sissy were dating," I said. "In fact, at dinner last night, I would have never believed it was even possible."

"We're not dating. She made that abundantly clear tonight. When she asked me to the dinner party last night, thinking she was irritating her mother instead of pleasing her, I realized that there was more there between the two of us than I knew. After spending some of the day with her today, I knew that I'd been overlooking someone right under my nose all along. She felt it too. It was obvious to me that she wanted to go out with me tonight when she agreed to have dinner, and then we had that spat. I tried to make it work, but evidently it's not going to happen between the two of us."

Jake looked at him sternly and asked, "So you're just going to give up?"

Gregory looked surprised by my husband's tone and his words. As a matter of fact, so was I. "You heard her, Jake. She doesn't believe me when I tell her that I'm over Shannon, and I don't know how to make her see that it's all ancient history."

"Let me ask you something, Gregory. Are you serious about her?"

"I think we could be amazing together," he said softly.

"Then go after her!"

"Do you mean right now?" Gregory asked as he looked in the direction she'd just gone.

"Yes. No. I mean from this moment forward, you should do your best to woo her, man. What have you got to lose but the prospect of being without her? If she's worth being with, then she's worth fighting for. Or are you afraid of a little humiliation?"

"No, I can take that," he said. "You're right. I'm *not* going to just give up. Hank can hide like some kind of petulant child, but I'm a grown man."

"Then start acting like it," Jake said.

The attorney nodded, and then, talking to himself again, he said, "I'll get some flowers on the way. She loves daisies. Maybe some candy, too."

As he drove off, I looked at my husband in surprise. "Now who's the matchmaker? Haven't you accused me in the past of doing exactly what you just did?"

"Guilty as charged," he said as he walked over and put his arms around me. After kissing me soundly, he pulled back and said, "Do you have a problem with that?"

"No, sir. I'm still not sure what just happened, though."

"I just can't bear to see someone let life pass them by, you know? If Gregory fails to convince Sissy that they belong together, then at least he tried, but doing nothing is absolutely the *worst* thing he can do. If he doesn't at least try, he'll never forgive himself. I have a hunch Eloise saw that spark there, too. That's why she warned Sissy not to invite Gregory.

It had nothing to do with our search for Hank. She was doing a little matchmaking herself."

"You could be right. In fact, she said something to that effect to me earlier today," I said. "Boy, *nobody* is who they seem to be at first glance here, are they?"

"Very rarely," he admitted. "Are you ready to go back to the guest cottage?"

"I am," I said as I stretched. "It's been a long day."

"And tomorrow is going to be longer than today was," Jake said as he started to drive us back to the A-frame.

"Why do you say that?"

"I don't know. Call it a hunch, but I don't think Hank Sandler is going to be able to stay in hiding much longer. The walls are starting to close in on him."

"In what way?"

"We know that Hump has been helping him, and if your suspicions are correct, he's been in contact with his mother, too. Something is going to happen one way or the other tomorrow or the next day at the latest."

"And if it doesn't?"

"Then we're going to make it happen," Jake answered.

"How do we do that?" I asked, using 'we' as if I were included in his plan.

"We start putting pressure on Hump, on Eloise, on Delia, and on anyone else we suspect of helping Hank Sandler. If he has no place to run, he might just decide this has gone on long enough. As a matter of fact, I'm going to talk to Chief Vickers first thing in the morning and push him to start pressing those three tomorrow."

"If you push Eloise too hard you might get us evicted, you know," I said.

"We can deal with that if and when it happens, can't we?" he asked me with a grin as he pulled up in front of the guesthouse.

"I told you before that I'd sleep in the truck if I had to, and I meant it," I told him with a grin as I squeezed his arm. "If I'm with you, that's all I need. Well, maybe a pillow. And a blanket—it gets chilly at night. Actually, a tent would be nice now that I think about it."

Jake started laughing, which had been my goal all along. "Suzanne, I love being married to my best friend."

"Right back at you. Now I'm going to go in and take another shower before bed while I still have the chance. If I'm going to be evicted in the morning, I want to take full advantage of the place tonight."

"That sounds like a plan to me," Jake said.

The next morning after Jake took off with Chief Vickers, I decided to head into town to see how Harley was doing. I grabbed a bite of toast and a quick cup of coffee, thinking that I might sample one of his donuts, purely out of respect for my fellow donut maker of course. Well, that wasn't the *only* reason, but even then, my breakfast wouldn't last me long. Then again, I wasn't afraid of an early lunch. It felt good having a bit of home here in Parsons Pond, and being in a donut shop was exactly what that felt like to me.

I drove the truck down into town and parked in front of the shop.

My first moment of unease came when I realized that there were no other vehicles parked there.

The second was that the lights were out and the CLOSED sign hung in the door.

The third and final one was the handwritten sign in the door.

*I want to thank my customers for their loyal support, but unfortunately, Donut Land will not reopen. Anyone interested in buying the business should contact Maggie Blaine at Blaine Realty.*

*Harley Haskins*

I called Harley's number, but he didn't pick up. What was going on here? I decided to walk down the street to the realty office. I'd noticed the sign coming in the day before, and Maggie Blaine was quite possibly the only one who could give me an answer to what was really going on.

Her photo on the front door showed a young, vibrant redhead somewhere in her early thirties, but the woman sitting at the desk in front was at least twenty years older, though the resemblance was clear enough. "Is Maggie here?" I asked her, thinking that she must work with her mother.

"I'm Maggie," she said brightly. "How may I help you?"

"You're Maggie?" I asked, confused by her admission. Was it possible that her mother's name was Maggie as well?

"I know," she said with a smile. "It's like a reverse Dorian Gray, isn't it? Everybody keeps telling me that I need to update my sign, but I love the way I looked back then."

"I think you look pretty terrific now," I said earnestly. Though it was true she was older, with that age had come a softness to her features that made me want to trust her more than that young woman in the photograph.

"Thank you, but I own a mirror."

"Don't sell yourself short," I said. "I'd be more inclined to buy something from *you* than I would that woman in the picture."

"Well then, you're in luck, because I'd be delighted to sell you whatever you're interested in."

"I shouldn't have misled you. I'm not in the market for anything but information."

Maggie didn't seem put off by my admission. "If I can help, I'll do my best. Who knows? You might want to buy something later."

"Why is Harley selling his donut shop?" I asked.

Maggie nodded. "You must be Suzanne."

"How on earth did you know that?" I asked her.

"Harley told me about you yesterday," she replied. "He thought about calling you to tell you what was going on, but he was afraid you might not understand."

"What's to understand? He's selling his place and quitting the donut business." I took a deep breath as I asked, "You don't happen to know how things with Delia went, do you? Did something happen between them yesterday?"

"You must know Harley *really* well," she said without really answering my question.

"We just met yesterday," I admitted.

"I'm not sure that matters all that much," she said. "Yes, Delia was the reason he put the shop on the market."

"They're splitting up, aren't they?" I asked glumly. What had I done, meddling in the poor man's life and possibly ruining it?

"Quite the contrary. Harley said that since they cleared the air between them, things have never been better. They're selling the business and moving to the beach, which is where they both really want to be in the first place. I got them in touch with a friend of mine on the Outer Banks who is showing them properties even as we speak."

"Did Harley seem happy about the decision?" I asked her.

"He was over the moon." She lowered her voice even though we were alone in the office. "You've heard the rumors about Delia and Hank Sandler, haven't you?"

"I might have heard something to that effect," I admitted reluctantly.

"Well, it turns out that it simply wasn't true. She and Hank were friends and nothing more. When Harley confronted her, she broke down and confessed that she was miserable in Parsons Pond and needed a change of scenery desperately. Evidently she pled with Harley to sell the business and come with her so they could start over, and he didn't even hesitate. He really loves her, and for the first time since they were first together, I honestly believe that she loves him right back. Who would have thought it would turn out that way?"

"I'm glad for him if he's really happy," I said. Maybe my interfering had helped after all.

"Since you already own one donut shop, why not start your own chain?" the realtor suggested. "Harley told me all about Donut Hearts. You could have his old place for a song, and I'm sure you'd be able to make it a success."

"You don't even know me," I told Maggie, marveling at her ability to turn our conversation into a sales pitch.

"Maybe not, but I've tasted your donuts, and I'm sure they are winners. What do you say?"

"I say I'd better stick to one shop," I said. "Thanks for the offer, though."

"I'm here if you change your mind."

"I won't, but I appreciate it," I said.

She smiled, clearly undaunted by my refusal. "That's why I'm here. Have a good day, Suzanne."

"You too, Maggie."

I wandered around town in the overcast gloom for the rest of the morning, popping into shops as I came to them. There was the standard gamut of small-town businesses all along the main drag, but one shop in particular caught my eye. It featured a host of animals out front, colorfully painted metal art objects that featured just about every creature known to man. Some were stationary, but most had parts that spun at the slightest hint of a breeze. I couldn't help myself. I walked inside.

There were ceramic animals besides the metal ones, cardboard ones, small die-cast critters, and wooden cutouts, too. A lovely older woman in her eighties was behind the front desk, painting a wooden zebra and laughing.

"What's so funny?" I asked her.

"I was just thinking of a name for him," she admitted. "I name them all, you know. It makes them more personal."

I looked at a nearby metal pig that stood more than five feet tall and was wearing a frilly evening dress, but if she had a name, I couldn't find it. "Who is this?"

"That's Piggerella, of course," she said. "See the one glass slipper?"

I hadn't noticed it before, but sure enough, the pig was wearing only one slipper. "That's too cute. And the zebra you are working on?"

"He's a little shy about telling me so far," she admitted. "No worries, though. I'll coax it out of him before long. That's a fact." The woman must have realized how she'd sounded. "You must think I'm off my rocker."

"As a matter of fact, if you're crazy, you're *my* kind of crazy," I said with a smile.

"I'm Josephine," she said as she offered me a paint-spattered hand.

I took it without hesitation. "I'm Suzanne."

She smiled. "Are you in the market for a new friend?"

"I'd love it," I said, "but I'm afraid I won't be in town long enough to make any new ones."

She laughed that golden laugh of hers. "I didn't mean me, dear. I was talking about someone from my menagerie."

"Maybe," I said as I looked around the shop. I spotted a pair of small ceramic cats, one black and one gray, but I couldn't find names anywhere on them, either. "What are their names?"

"That's Shadow and Midnight," she answered promptly.

"Am I missing something?" I asked.

"What do you mean?"

"I don't see their names written anywhere on them," I admitted.

"Oh, they don't like their names written down for everyone to see," she said conspiratorially. "What if someone buys them and wants to call them something else? No, those are their private names just between us."

"Well, I think these two are named perfectly already," I said as I picked them up and walked to the desk. "I'd love to take them home with me."

"And I'm sure they'd love being there," she said. She carefully wrapped both cats and put them in a bag after I paid her for them. I knew just the spot in the donut shop kitchen for them, and I thought it would be nice having a little company on the days I worked at Donut Hearts alone.

"Have a lovely day, Suzanne," she said as I made my way out the door.

"You too, Josephine."

I tucked the cats safely into a bin behind my seat in the truck and felt my stomach rumble. It was time to get something to eat, and I knew exactly where I wanted to go.

Chapter 15

THE PUB WASN'T NEARLY as crowded as it had been the day before. I got a good table and was just about to order when I heard laughter coming from the office. The door was open, so naturally I peeked inside. To my surprise and delight, I saw Gregory there with Sissy, and evidently they'd found some common ground after all. I heard him say, "I've got to get back to the office. If you need me, I'm just a phone call away."

"For business or something more personal?" she asked him with a grin.

"For business, it might take an hour, but for something personal, I'll be here in three minutes."

"I like your priorities, sir," she said as she kissed him soundly. "Now shoo. I have work to do."

"Yes, ma'am. See you tonight?"

"Absolutely," she replied, her face flushed with joy.

Gregory grinned at me as he approached my table. "Tell your husband that he's a genius," he said as he almost skipped out of the pub.

Sissy must have noticed him stopping and talking to me. "What did Gregory have to say?" she asked as she approached.

"Just how happy he was," I improvised. After all, it wasn't my place to tell Sissy that Jake had been the one to goad Gregory into going after her the night before.

"Don't worry, Suzanne, Gregory told me all about your husband's conversation with him last night in the parking lot after I left. I'm not exactly sure what Jake said to him, but it was just what Gregory needed to hear."

"I'm glad you're giving him a chance," I said with a smile.

"What can I say? He wooed me," she answered as she turned to the waitress approaching. "Cynthia, give her whatever she wants on me."

"You don't have to do that," I protested.

"I don't have to, but I want to. Is Jake joining you?"

"No, sorry, he's working."

"A man still has to eat though, doesn't he?" my husband asked, stunning me with his presence.

Sissy didn't even hesitate as she kissed him on the cheek and hugged him. After a moment she pulled away and turned to me. "Sorry about that. I shouldn't have done that with another woman's husband."

"You have my permission just this once," I said with a smile. Her good humor was infectious.

"Not that I'm complaining, but what was that all about?" Jake asked as he sat down and joined me.

"Evidently the wooing part didn't take long. Gregory just left, and the two of them appear to be in a relationship already."

Jake looked pleased. "I'm glad."

"Not that I'm complaining, but what are you doing here?"

"Bo had some personal business to take care of, so he dropped me off here when we spotted my truck in the parking lot. Care for a lunch companion?"

"I'd love it," I admitted. "Sissy said whatever we get today is on the house, so order anything you'd like."

"She doesn't have to do that," Jake said with a frown.

I touched his arm lightly. "Let her, Jake. It's important to her."

"Okay then," he said as he studied the menu. After we both ordered our food and got our drinks, Jake asked, "Now where's this photo you were telling me about?"

"It's over here," I said as I stood and walked back to the place I'd spotted it the day before.

There was only one problem, though.

The picture was gone.

In its place was one of a little boy missing a few teeth, eating an ear of corn. "I don't understand," I said. "It was here yesterday."

"Maybe Sissy moved it," Jake said.

"Let's go ask her," I replied.

"That's odd. I noticed there was a gap on the wall this morning," she admitted when we asked her about it. "It's a pretty prominent place, so I found a frame that fit the spot and threw that one up there instead."

"Do you have any idea who might have taken the picture?" Jake asked.

"Are you asking me about the photographer?" she inquired, clearly thinking it was an odd question. "I don't even know what the picture was of."

"It was your brother, Gregory, Bo, and Shannon the day they graduated from high school," I told her.

"I just figured that someone on the staff must have knocked it off the wall accidently last night," she said with a frown. "I didn't think it was any big deal, but that sounds like a photo I'd love to have myself. Let me make a few calls."

She did, and after a minute, she said, "No one remembers anything happening last night. It was there when Cora closed up, but it was gone when I got here this morning. How strange."

"Indeed," Jake said.

At that moment, our waitress came into the office. "Your food is ready. Should I put it on the table or take it back to the kitchen so they can keep it warm?"

"No, we'll eat now," Jake said.

"If you hear anything else about it, let us know, okay?" I asked her.

"I will. Is it important?"

"At this point, who knows? But I'd really like to know," I told her.

"So would I," Jake chimed in.

As we ate, I asked him, "What do you make of that?"

"I'm not entirely sure," he said as he took another bite of his rib eye sandwich. "Wow, you were right. This is amazing."

"My burger's great, too," I said, "and the fries are really tasty, too." I pointed a fry at him before I dipped it into catsup. "You never told me how your morning went. Did you have any luck pressuring the folks you were going to talk to?"

"Delia and Harley are gone," Jake said softly. "For good. I didn't want to tell you, but you have a right to know."

"I heard all about it. They're starting over at the Outer Banks," I told him as I ate the fry and then patted his hand. "It's okay. Being a donut maker isn't for everyone."

"I get that," he said. "If you ask me, it sounds like too much work."

"Like catching bad guys isn't?" I asked him with a laugh.

"You do that, too, Suzanne," he replied.

"So, if you didn't talk to Delia, did you at least pressure Mayor Humphries and Eloise Sandler?"

"Yes and no," Jake said between bites.

"You're going to have to do better than that, at least if you're at liberty to disclose it to me," I told him. "I'm too invested in this to keep my nose out of it anymore."

"Is that what you've been doing so far?" he asked with a smile.

"As much as I've been able to manage it," I replied with a shrug. "So, have we been evicted yet?"

"No, but that's more due to the fact that we couldn't find Eloise. Bo was a little reluctant to press the two most influential people in town, but after I convinced him to let me play 'bad cop,' he went along with it."

"Did you at least talk to the mayor?"

"We did," Jake admitted after taking another bite of his sandwich.

"And?" I asked.

"Well, it was kind of odd. I was under the impression that Hump and Bo had a good relationship, but he seemed to bristle every time the police chief asked him a question."

"Did he give you the same treatment?"

"He wasn't exactly happy with me, but it was warm sunshine and flower bouquets compared to how he acted around Chief Vickers. I think it's probably because he doesn't know me all that well, so I got some leeway. On the other hand, he's known Bo forever, so I'm sure it wasn't comfortable for him to be questioned so intently."

"Did it help?" I asked as I polished off my burger.

"Time will tell. We're going to speak with Eloise this afternoon, and then we'll see if our pressure produces any results."

"And if it doesn't?"

Jake sighed after he polished off his meal. "Then tomorrow, we ramp it up even more."

"So, things are about to get even *more* intense around here," I observed as Sissy approached our table.

"I'd say they were," he said softly, and then he turned to Sissy. "That was amazing. Are you sure we can't pay you for that meal? It was incredible."

"Your money isn't good here as long as you're in town," the new pub owner said with a smile. "And don't leave a tip, either."

"I can't do that," Jake protested as he reached for his wallet.

"Trust me, I already took care of Cynthia," she said.

"You tipped your own server for us?" I asked. "That was completely over the top."

"I didn't exactly tip her. I gave her a day off without pay, which is better for both of us and what she really wanted," Sissy said. "Now, who wants dessert?"

I was about to reach for the menu she was offering when Jake said, "Thanks, but we're stuffed."

I smiled at Sissy. "It was excellent, though. Thank you again."

"It was my pleasure," she said.

As we were walking out, I asked Jake, "You're too full for dessert? Since when?"

"Suzanne, she just bought us lunch," he admitted. "I wasn't about to stick her for dessert, too."

I squeezed his arm. "That's what I thought. So, are you *really* full?"

"I really am," he said. "How about you?"

"I'm good for now. So, is Chief Vickers picking you up here?"

"No, I'm supposed to meet him at the police station," Jake said as he pointed up the road.

"Do you want a ride?"

"It's just a few blocks, and I could use the exercise," he said.

"As a matter of fact, so could I," I admitted. "I'll walk you there and then come back for the truck later."

"You don't have to do that, Suzanne."

"What's the matter, Jake? Tired of my company already?" I asked him with a grin.

"Never," he said as he took my hand in his.

The weather had taken a turn for the worst with thick clouds and fog rolling into town, and the air was damp and heavy from it, but that didn't spoil our walk together.

When we got to the police station though, the police chief's car was gone.

Where was Chief Vickers?

Was he still on his personal errand, or had something cracked in the case of the missing developer?

"Where's the chief?" Jake asked the front-desk officer. "I was supposed to meet him here five minutes ago."

"He told me to tell you that he's taking the afternoon off for some personal business."

"Now? In the middle of an investigation?" Jake asked him.

"Evidently Ginny had some kind of breakdown," the cop said softly. "He said that she's more important than finding Hank Sandler right now, at least to him."

"Fine," Jake said. "If he changes his mind and decides to work this afternoon after all, have him give me a call, okay? He's got my number."

"Mr. Bishop, the man's entitled to a life," the officer explained. "Ginny's all that he's got left in the world."

"I get it," Jake said, softening a bit. "Thanks, Davis."

"You bet," the man said.

"Well, suddenly I'm in need of an investigating partner," Jake told me once we were back outside.

"I happen to know an enthusiastic donut maker who would love to help," I said.

"I thought Harley was on the Outer Banks looking at houses?" Jake asked me with the hint of a grin.

"He is, but maybe if you start walking now, you'll be there by next week, and you can ask yourself." I started back toward the truck and I'd made it a hundred feet before my husband caught up with me. It really was a dreary day, and the fog and mist had gotten worse. I didn't envy anyone who had to be out driving in it.

"Hey, I was just teasing. I'd *love* your help," Jake said.

I grinned at him, and after sticking my tongue out at my dearly beloved, I said, "I'm not sure I want to help you now." That was a bald-faced lie and we both knew it. There was nothing in the world I wanted more than to investigate this case with my husband.

"Are you really going to make me beg?" he asked.

"I would, but it's too dreary out to do that." Showing the enthusiasm that I'd felt all along, I added, "I'll even let you drive."

"I have your permission to drive my own truck? You're quite a special gal, Suzanne."

"Is that sarcasm, Jake?" I asked him sweetly.

"No, ma'am. I mean it. To prove it, I'll let *you* drive *me* around."

I looked around. "In this soup? No thank you. If I had my Jeep, I'd be happy to, but I'd rather not take a chance and wreck your truck."

"I understand that. Let's go get it, and then we can figure out our next move."

We were back in the parking lot of the pub when I spotted a familiar face, especially one I hadn't been expecting to see.

"Ginny, are you okay?" I asked the police chief's sister.

"I'm doing better. Thanks for asking," she said brightly. "Listen, I'm sorry about last night. I was feeling a bit lost, but there's nothing like a good night's sleep to help give a little perspective."

"Where's Bo?" Jake asked. "Is he right behind you?"

"Bo?" she asked, clearly puzzled. "I'm surprised he's not with you. I thought you were trying to find Hank together."

"We are," Jake said. "We must have just gotten our signals crossed."

"That happens to the best of us," Ginny said. "Well, I'd better get back to work. Tell my big brother that I'm better the next time you see him, okay?"

"We will," I told her.

Once we were in Jake's truck, I asked, "What do you suppose that was all about? Why would he lie and tell people that he was taking time off to be with his sister when she's clearly just fine?"

"It's obvious, isn't it?" Jake asked as he started driving a familiar route. "He knows where Hank is, and he's determined to bring him in himself."

"Would he do that to you?" I asked as Jake started creeping along. He couldn't go more than ten miles an hour without risking hitting something in the fog.

"Suzanne, he needs to prove to the world that he's every bit as good a police chief as Harley was. I get it. I don't have to like it, but at least I can understand it."

"Jake Bishop, nobody's ever outshone you in your life," I said. "Just when I was starting to like the man, he pulls something like this. What are we going to do about it?"

"Well, we can't very well search the streets of this town when we're half blinded by this miserable fog, but I'm not sure we have to. There was just one more person we were going to push today, remember?"

"You think he's at Eloise's house?" I asked him.

"It's the only place I can think of that makes any sense. You heard Eloise say on the phone that whoever was on the other end had to grow up. I'm willing to bet Hank came to her for help when we found him at the mayor's house and Bo Vickers got wind of it."

"What are we going to do when we get there?" I asked him. "Assuming that we *do* get there. Slow down, Jake. You're driving too fast."

"Suzanne, I'm barely creeping as it is," he said as another car suddenly came out of the fog and nearly hit us.

Jake slammed on his horn and took quick evasive action, which was most likely the *only* thing that saved us from getting hit head-on. "That wasn't my fault! That idiot was in the middle of the road!"

"I know. Should we wait until this fog clears?"

"I can drop you off somewhere if you're uncomfortable making the trip, but I'm going to Eloise Sandler's house right now," Jake said. I knew he hated the idea that Chief Vickers had played him for the fool.

"No, I'm going with you," I said. It was the way I wanted it. If something did happen to Jake, I wanted—no, I needed—to be right there with him.

"Are you sure about that?" he looked over at me and grinned as he asked.

I gave him two thumbs up as I said, "I am, but keep watching the road."

"What road?" he asked, and I could swear he laughed a little as he said it.

Apparently I'd married a lunatic.

Well, to be fair, so had he.

## Chapter 16

AS JAKE DROVE, I HAD some time to think. From Jake's perspective, I could see how he might believe that Chief Vickers was trying to hog the glory of finding Hank Sandler himself. It made sense his way, but as we continued on in the fog, another thought struck me, something much darker.

"Jake, if I tell you what I'm thinking, will you hear me out and give me the benefit of the doubt before you make up your mind that I'm crazy?"

"Being crazy isn't necessarily a bad thing," Jake said. "Go on. I'll listen."

"What if we're reading this entire situation wrong?"

I could tell that he wanted to say something, but instead, he replied, "I'm listening. What's your theory?"

"What if Hank disappeared for a very good reason?" I asked. "It had something to do with Shannon, but not what we think." Before he could stop me, I told him the cascade of thoughts I'd just had that told me there was at least a chance I was right. "Let's go back in time to when Shannon disappeared. I've been thinking about why someone would take that photograph, and then it hit me. I noticed something on her wrist. At first I thought it was just a shadow on the photograph, but what if it was a bruise? I've seen those before where someone's been grabbed against their will. It's even happened to me."

"Do you think *Hank* did it? Did they have a fight when he found out she was leaving him the next day?" Jake asked.

"No. The truth is that I don't think Shannon had any intention at all of leaving Parsons Pond," I said.

"You think somebody killed her that night, don't you?" Jake asked. "I've been playing with that idea myself. It could explain why Hank disappeared all of a sudden recently. Somebody clearly found *something* in Shannon's bedroom the night we found muddy tracks going to her room. It could be that he was worried that it pointed to him, and he got scared and ran."

"I don't think Hank killed Shannon, Jake," I said. "I think Bo Vickers did."

## Chapter 17

"BO? WHY WOULD HE KILL her?"

"Everybody in town has been telling us that *all* of the guys were in love with Shannon Bridger," I said. "In that photo, Bo had his arm around her tightly, but she was holding her diploma in the hand that was closest to him. No one else was holding anything, Jake. The rest of them had their arms around each other."

"That doesn't make him guilty of murder, Suzanne," Jake said reasonably.

"Let's suppose for one second that it does," I said. "Think about it. Bo was in love with her, and you told me yourself that he has a temper. Let's say he got drunk that night and made a pass at her. She rejected him, and he killed her. Maybe it was even an accident. He got rid of the body and then made it look like she'd left town, but what if Shannon left an entry in her diary that told a different story? Sissy told me that Shannon kept hers in that hiding spot sometimes. Everybody believed the story, but Bo couldn't hang around a town where he'd killed the only girl he ever loved. He joined the Army to get away, and he didn't come back to Parsons Pond until his folks died and his sister needed him."

"So you're saying that *Hank* found the diary?" Jake asked me, still studying the road carefully so we'd make it to our destination in one piece.

"He was flipping the house for his mother," I reminded him. "Let's say he found the diary, but before he could decide what to do with it, someone came to the house. He jammed it back in its hiding place without knowing that we'd soon be staying there. When he thought we were going to be there awhile, he broke back in and took it. Thus the muddy footprints."

"But why didn't he go to the police? I mean the State Troopers, or at least someone above Bo."

"Maybe he didn't think the diary would be enough evidence," I said, "or maybe he wanted the man to pay for his crime by his own hand. Remember, Shannon was the love of Hank's life, and if Bo took her away from him forever, it might have been enough to push a man everyone has been telling us is still despondent all of these years later over the edge. Hank could have taken that photograph himself to confront Bo with the image of all of them together one last time."

I waited in silence as Jake drove. Saying it all out loud somehow made it more real to me. I could be wrong, but I could see Bo reacting the way I'd described it back then, and Hank, from what I'd heard of him, could easily do what he was doing now. Had he laid a trap for Bo at his mother's place, *wanting* to be caught, or at least confronted by the police chief? Was he getting his own slice of revenge for a crime that had happened so many years before? I knew that none of my evidence would hold up in a court of law, but then, that wasn't my job.

I was looking for the truth.

Jake finally decided to speak as we neared the Sandler house.

Instead of pulling into her long driveway, he parked at the foot of ours, well within walking distance of the house but still leaving us a chance to go in undetected.

"What do you think? Am I wrong about everything?" I asked him.

"I don't think so," Jake said as he reached for his gun. "I just hope we got here in time. If you're right, there's a good chance there's about to be another murder."

## Chapter 18

AS WE WALKED THROUGH the dense fog toward the house, I started hearing voices. It was amazing how the weather could affect the way sound travelled. Everything that was being said sounded as though it was just a few feet in front of us instead of so many yards. Jake and I hurried our pace as I heard a man's voice that had to be Hank's say, "Shannon wrote it all down in her diary, Bo! You can deny it all you want, but you'd been making passes at her for weeks. She was going to tell me the night we graduated. Is that when you killed her, Bo? Were you trying to shut her up?"

Bo Vickers spoke next. There was a toughness, even a meanness in his voice as he said, "She was a tease, and you know it. She wanted *me*, Hank, not you. You saw how she acted around me."

"Bo, that was her nature! She flirted with everybody."

"Well, she shouldn't have done it with me. When did you find out?"

"The minute before I disappeared," Hank said.

"You didn't run far, did you? Why did the mayor help you?"

"He owed me one," Hank said.

"Did you tell him what you found?" Bo asked.

Hank waited too long to answer. "No."

"You're lying," the chief of police said, and I knew that Mayor Humphries and possibly his wife were both in jeopardy now, too. "How about your mother?"

"Leave her out of this, Bo! She doesn't know a thing."

"Sissy?" he asked.

If we let Bo escape, there was about to be a rash of homicides in this sleepy little town.

"Don't go after my family! Leave them alone!" Hank yelled at him.

After a short pause, Chief Vickers said, "You should be more worried about yourself right now."

Hank's voice was softer as he asked, "What really happened the night we graduated, Bo? I know we'd all been drinking. Did things get out of hand? It might not even have been your fault. You can tell me."

"I'm not afraid of you, Hank, even if you are pointing a gun at me. I've got one too, remember, and I'm not afraid to use mine."

"Then shoot me or answer my question," Hank said.

How far away were they? We were hurrying up the drive, but it seemed as though the voices were coming more from behind the house now than in front of it. Could the confrontation be happening near the spot where I'd found Eloise earlier? I touched Jake's arm. "This way."

"The house is over there," he whispered back.

"Trust me."

He nodded, and we started off in our changed direction. I could see Jake, if just barely, and I realized that he had his weapon out, too. I started wishing for that golf club or my softball bat. Shoot, I would have even taken a rock or a heavy branch, but I was defenseless.

"Fine," Bo said angrily. "We'll do it your way. She turned me down one too many times. When I tried to kiss her, she pushed me away, playing her games again. I shoved her in anger, and she lost her footing. She tripped and hit her head on a rock. I didn't mean to do it. It was an accident." The words almost came out in a flood of relief, and I wondered how Bo had managed to deal with the weight of what he'd done for all of those years.

"Did she die instantly?" Hank asked, his voice shrouded in a soft whimper of tears.

"Yes," Bo said after hesitating a moment, getting control of his emotions again. I wondered if he was lying even now.

"What did you do with her body?"

"It's in the swamp by her house," Bo said dully. "I put her in a heavy tarp and weighted it down."

"She didn't leave me after all," Hank said softly as we got closer.

"In a way, she left us all. I couldn't stand being here anymore, so I joined up and got out. I kept waiting for a tap on my shoulder, but it never came. My folks died, and Ginny begged me to come back. What choice did I have? I didn't mean to do it, Hank, but I'm not going to spend the rest of my life paying for an accident that happened a long time ago."

"Let's go to Jake Bishop, Bo," Hank pled. "He can help us get through this. They'll be able to prove that you didn't mean to do it. It's going to be all right."

"I'm sorry, but that ship has sailed," Bo said. "There's no way I'm going to deal with it now."

"Then what are you going to do, shoot me?"

In response, a gun went off.

Evidently that was exactly what Chief of Police Bo Vickers did.

"Jake, don't," I said as I tried to restrain my husband.

"Hank might still be alive! Stay here!"

I knew that was the smart thing to do, but I couldn't bring myself to do it. I gave Jake ten seconds as a head start, and then I ran after him into the swirling fog.

## Chapter 19

"DROP THE WEAPON," I heard Jake yell out ahead of me.

There was another loud bang, and then I heard footsteps running toward me! Bo Vickers's voice called out as he neared me, "I don't want to kill you too, Jake."

I started to run away from the man, but like Shannon years before me, I tripped and fell just as Bo could see me. He yanked me up by my wrist hard enough to bruise it and pulled me toward him. The hot steel of the gun in his hands pressed against my chest. "Stop! I've got your wife!"

"Just take it easy, Bo. We can work this out," Jake said from ten or twelve feet away. I could barely make him out now, but I hoped that Bo couldn't. "It doesn't have to end this way."

"I don't really see another way out of this," Bo said calmly. "I may be on my way out, but I'm not going out alone."

I felt the pressure of the gun increase, and I knew he was about to shoot me first and then go after my husband.

I punched above my head backward, where I figured Bo's face was, and the strike met with a satisfying smack. I didn't know if I hit his nose, which was my target, or one of his eyes, which would have been fine with me too, but I'd clearly struck home. I'd seen the move performed on a self-defense video, but at the time, I'd prayed that I'd never have to try it myself.

Bo's grip on me eased for just a moment as the shock and pain from my sudden attack hit him, and I broke free. I thought about grappling with him for the gun, but he was too strong for me, and we both knew it.

"Jake, I'm free!" I screamed as I dropped to the ground.

My husband came out of nowhere and hit Bo Vickers harder than I'd ever seen a man hit before. The police chief collapsed in on himself as though he were a marionette whose strings had been cut, and I was afraid that Jake had killed him with a single blow.

Once my husband had retrieved the chief's gun and handcuffed the unconscious man, he found me in a break in the fog. His hug was so tight I could barely breathe, but I didn't protest.

"You didn't shoot him," I said.

"I couldn't take the chance. I didn't know where you were, and I wasn't going to risk hitting you. Are you okay?"

"I'm a little bruised and battered, but I'll be fine. Did he kill Hank?"

"I don't know," Jake said. He pulled out his cell phone and dialed a quick number. "I need backup right now," he said and gave Eloise's address. "Send a squad car and an ambulance. There's a man down."

"Did you call the Parsons Pond police department?" I asked him after he hung up.

"No. When I got into town, I checked in with an old friend with the state police. I do it every time I work a case out of town."

"Jake, did you suspect Bo from the start?" I asked him incredulously.

My husband shook his head. The fog was finally starting to lift, almost as though on command. "Not hardly. You just never know when you might need a friend nearby."

Bo started to stir, and Jake reached down and jerked him up by his secured wrists. "Hey, take it easy," the chief of police complained.

"Move," Jake said as he shoved him in the back toward Hank Sandler.

When we got to the clearing, the fog was definitely dissipating. Eloise Sandler was already there, kneeling on the ground and cradling her son's head in her lap.

"How is he doing?" Jake asked calmly.

"I don't know," she said through her tears. "The bullet appears to have only grazed him, and I've got a scarf pressed to the wound to stop the bleeding, but I can't get him to answer me. Did you shoot my son, Jake?" She asked the question with the fire of an angry mother.

"No. He did," Hank said, stirring as he pointed toward Bo Vickers. "If Jake and Suzanne hadn't come along when they did, he would have finished the job, too."

"Then I'll deal with you later," she said as she stared at the police chief.

Bo Vickers had the nerve to laugh. "Eloise, if anything good has come of this mess, it's that I don't have to be afraid of you anymore. You don't have any power over me."

"Don't bet on it," she snapped.

"Take it easy, Mom. It's going to be okay," Hank said, oddly enough trying to calm his mother even though he'd been the one who'd just been shot.

"Did someone call an ambulance?" she asked us.

"One's on its way," I said as we heard the first sirens in the background.

"That will be my friend with the state police, too," Jake said. "We'll meet them and send the ambulance back to you."

"Thank you for saving my son," Eloise said.

"It was our pleasure, Eloise. Suzanne played a big part in it, too," Jake answered before he turned to me. "I'll be right back."

"You'd better," I said. I wanted to hug him again, but he was standing too close to the handcuffed killer, so I decided that it could wait.

"It appears that I owe you my thanks as well," Eloise said after Jake and his prisoner were gone.

"I'm just glad it turned out okay," I said.

"It didn't though, did it?" Hank asked from where he lay. "Shannon's been dead all these years, and I thought she walked out on me. She hasn't deserved any of the things I've thought about her."

"I'm so sorry, Son," Eloise said as she touched his shoulder lightly.

"It's okay, Mom," Hank said. "Knowing is better than not knowing. Maybe now I can get past what happened and have a life of my own. I've made some bad decisions over the years, but that's all going to change. Getting shot changes you."

The EMTs could see us now, which just showed how fast the fog was really starting to clear. As they wrapped Hank's head and transferred him to the gurney, Eloise was never more than a few inches away from her prodigal son. I walked back with them as they rolled him to the ambulance, and I was standing there alone after they drove away. Jake was with his former state police colleague, and Bo Vickers was sitting in the back of the cruiser, staring ahead at nothing.

I hoped he had a long life sitting in a cell doing the exact same thing. Shannon's murder might have been an accident, but then again, he could have scrubbed the memory of what had really happened and replaced it with a story that shed a more favorable light on his behavior all those years ago. At the very least, he'd broken quite a few laws, and tonight, he'd added attempted murder to the list. If they counted him grabbing me at gunpoint, he could add kidnapping to the list of charges, but no matter how it washed out, Bo Vickers was finished.

How many lives had he ruined in the process, though? Shannon and Hank weren't his only victims. Shannon's parents had surely been cursed, as well as anyone else that bright point of light's life had touched.

I knew Hank would have a rough go of it for a while despite his pledge to start a new life, but at least he'd have the chance to see what there was out there for him once enough time passed. He might never be the same man he'd been the day they'd graduated from high school, but at least now he knew the truth, and that counted for a great deal.

As for me, I couldn't wait to get back to the quiet life of April Springs, if you could call my life there quiet.

At least it was familiar, a home where I belonged, where the people I loved lived and worked and played.

It was more than I could ask for, and I vowed never to take it for granted.

Chapter 20

"ARE YOU *sure* you don't mind going back until morning?" Jake asked me as we settled into the guesthouse that evening.

"I'm positive," I said. "Now that everything is wrapped up, maybe we can have a quiet night in a luxury vacation home before we head back to our old life."

He snuggled closer to me on the couch as we sat in front of the fire. It was barely cool enough for one, but I didn't care if I had to open the windows and let a fresh breeze in. I was determined to enjoy the ambience of the place to the fullest.

"It's not such a bad life, is it?" he asked as he stretched a bit in place.

"I wouldn't trade it for anything in the world," I said.

"I wouldn't, either. Would you mind if we made a quick stop in Raleigh on the way back home tomorrow? I haven't seen my sister and her kids in a while, and it might be nice to pop in on them."

"Sounds good to me. Should we stop along the way and get presents for them?"

Jake laughed. "No, I don't want to spoil them. Besides, seeing us should be present enough."

"We'll stop along the way before we get there," I answered.

"Whatever you say," he answered contentedly.

I felt Jake nodding off beside me in the warmth, and I considered waking him up, but I decided to let him sleep a little longer. He'd had an exhausting time of it, and as a matter of fact, so had I. I was sorry I hadn't gotten a chance to know Hank but even sorrier that I'd never get to meet Shannon Bridger. From the sound of it, she would have been a good person to know, and she surely hadn't deserved the fate she'd met so many years ago, but at least we were leaving Parsons Pond better than we'd found it. Harley was reconnecting with his wife, Delia, Gregory and Sissy were exploring the possibilities of a new romance together, and even Hank might have the chance to finally put the past behind him.

All in all, it had been a positive experience, but the next time Jake got a case away from home, I was going to let him work it solo.

These vacations were just too stressful for me, and I knew I'd be better off doing what I did: making donuts and being there for my family and friends if and when they needed me.

It was my life, a good life, the *best* life I could have ever asked for.

RECIPES

# Easy Donuts

I use this recipe when I want to make a good basic drop donut. I've found that the benefit of dropping dough into the hot oil is that I don't have to fiddle with cutters or rolling pins. All I need are two table-spoons, one to scoop the batter and one to push it off into the hot oil, and I'm ready to go. They make the most interesting shapes, at least to me.

This donut requires an actual recipe, so they're the most difficult donuts to make in this particular book, but they really aren't that hard to create at all.

You can top these with whatever you'd like, from powdered sugar to vanilla glaze to a dusting of cocoa powder to a drizzle of honey. Sometimes the most creative part of the donut is what you decide to put over it. Play with it, and remember, it should be fun or you shouldn't do it (unlike paying taxes, unless you happen to enjoy that).

Have fun!

Ingredients

1 1/2 cups all-purpose flour (bleached or unbleached)

1/2 teaspoon baking soda

1/2 teaspoon baking powder

1/4 teaspoon nutmeg

Dash of salt

1 cup buttermilk

1/2 cup milk (2% or whole milk will also do)

1/2 cup granulated white sugar

1 teaspoon vanilla

1 whole egg, beaten

Directions

Heat some canola oil to 360°F while you mix the batter.

In a medium bowl, sift the flour, baking soda, baking powder, nutmeg, and salt together.

In a larger bowl, mix the buttermilk, milk, sugar, vanilla, and beaten egg together.

Slowly add the dry ingredients to the wet, mixing as you go.

When the ingredients are incorporated, take a tablespoon of batter and rake it into the fryer with another tablespoon. If the dough doesn't rise soon, gently nudge it with a chopstick, being careful not to splatter the oil.

After 2 minutes, flip the donuts, frying for another minute on the other side. These times may vary given too many factors to count, so keep a close eye on them so they don't burn.

Add whatever topping you choose while they're still warm, or eat them as they are!

Makes about a dozen small donuts.

# Even Easier Donuts

I call these my desperation donuts. When I haven't been to the store for a while and I'm missing some of my favorite ingredients, I'll make these in a pinch. Are they the best donuts you've ever had in your life? I would be shocked if they were, but they're still fried treats, tasty enough for what they are, so what's not to like about that?

Like I said in the title, they are certainly easy enough to make with some rather inexpensive ingredients, so honestly, what do you have to lose? To jazz them up, try some of the toppings suggestions above.

Ingredients

1/2 cup boxed biscuit flour

1/2 cup milk (or water if you don't have milk on hand)

1 tablespoon white granulated sugar

1 teaspoon cinnamon

Directions

Heat the canola oil to 350°F while you mix the batter.

In a medium-sized bowl, mix the biscuit flour, milk, sugar, and cinnamon together.

When the ingredients are incorporated, take a tablespoon of batter and rake it into the fryer with another spoon. If the dough doesn't rise quickly, gently nudge it with a long-handled utensil, being careful not to splatter oil.

After 2 minutes, flip the donut drops and let them fry for another minute on the other side.

Makes 6 to 8 small donuts.

# The Easiest Donuts You'll Ever Make

OKAY, WHEN I'M REALLY desperate, I make these donuts. Shhhh! The biggest surprise to me the first time I made these was how honestly good they were! They are tasty treats that deserve more praise then their humble origins suggest, and if you don't want to tell anyone what you made these donuts with as a base, your secret is safe with me.

I like to keep a tube of canned biscuits on hand for when I want a treat but I don't want to do much work to get it.

Ever have one of those days? Or even weeks, maybe? I know I do, so don't apologize.

They're still homemade in the strictest definition of the word. Well, at least they are as far as I'm concerned, and I won't tell if you don't.

Ingredients

1 canister refrigerated biscuits (Pillsbury Grands! Homestyle Buttermilk Biscuits work great, but I'm sure other canned biscuits would work, too.)

1/2 stick butter, salted or unsalted will work fine, softened (4 tablespoons)

3/4 cup granulated white sugar

1 1/2 tablespoons cinnamon

Directions

Heat the canola oil to 350°F while you make up these donuts. You'll be finished with your prep work before the oil heats up, or you're doing something wrong.

Open the canister of biscuits and gently form each individual biscuit into an oval.

In a small bowl, mix the softened butter, sugar, and cinnamon together and then put 1 to 2 tablespoons in the center of each oval.

Bring the dough up around the sides of the butter mixture and pinch the edges together tightly.

Drop the individual ovals into the oil. Fry for 3 to 5 minutes, turning halfway through.

Remove when they're golden brown, and you'll be greeted with five cinnamon smiles!

For an added treat, have more butter at hand to slather over the top if you're feeling really decadent!

Yield: 5 cinnamon toast sticks.

If you enjoy Jessica Beck Mysteries and you would like to be notified when the next book is being released, please visit our website at jessicabeckmysteries.net for valuable information about Jessica's books, and sign up for her new-releases-only mail blast.

Your email address will not be shared, sold, bartered, traded, broadcast, or disclosed in any way. There will be no spam from us, just a friendly reminder when the latest book is being released, and of course, you can drop out at any time.

Other Books by Jessica Beck

The Donut Mysteries
Glazed Murder
Fatally Frosted
Sinister Sprinkles
Evil Éclairs
Tragic Toppings
Killer Crullers
Drop Dead Chocolate
Powdered Peril
Illegally Iced
Deadly Donuts
Assault and Batter
Sweet Suspects
Deep Fried Homicide
Custard Crime
Lemon Larceny
Bad Bites
Old Fashioned Crooks
Dangerous Dough
Troubled Treats
Sugar Coated Sins
Criminal Crumbs
Vanilla Vices
Raspberry Revenge
Fugitive Filling
Devil's Food Defense
Pumpkin Pleas
Floured Felonies
Mixed Malice

Made in the USA
Columbia, SC
20 October 2020